Young Supreme Being:

Young Supreme Being:

The Hunt For Y. S. B.

Steven R. General

Please report any errors in text for corrections to the author at blueauthor.15@gmail.com
Thank you.

ISBN: 0993944752

Electronic Book ISBN: 9780993944758

Book ISBN: 9780993944765

TABLE OF CONTENTS

DEDICATION

For all the Sons and Daughters from the past,
For all the Sons and Daughters in the present,
But especially for all the Sons and Daughters
in the Future.

WE SAY UNTO YE

Genesis 6:5

"And GOD saw that the wickedness of man was great in the earth, and that every imagination of the thoughts of his heart was only evil continually."

CHAPTER 1

Scientists have been trying to unravel the mysteries of the human brain for centuries with only limited success. There is so much they do not know or understand and they likely will never know or understand the brain fully. Scientists have reported that a human being only uses about 7 to 10% of their brain and many can't help but wonder what is the remaining unused 90% to 93% for? They wonder what would be the limits of someone who managed to use 100% of their brain and would it even be possible to use the full extent of the brain … whatever that might be? Why is the brain not fully utilized? Is it to protect us from our lack of ethics, morality, greed and power without accountability? Will it be a future event when it suddenly appears? How could we utilize that lost amount of the human brain? When Albert Einstein died many wondered about his brain? Did he use more of his brain in some way … more than anyone else? There are certain clubs that are only open to very intelligent people. Some examples are the Mensa Society, the Intertel Society, the Triple Nine Society, the Prometheus Society and finally the Mega Society but they fail in comparison to a super intelligence. And how is intelligence really measured? Is it like the human body? Can we increase our brain's intelligence by exercising it or using some kind of magical drug or drugs to enhance it? Well the World is about to get the answer and that is a hell of a scary thing. And it started with the brain of a single Child born here on Earth.

In the beginning the rumors and the myths started to build and gain momentum slowly but it didn't take long before people realized that the rumors or myths were actually true. It started as a kind of urban legend that there lived a Child somewhere on the planet Earth that was different … so very different … like no one before. A Child that was different in the sense that there was a super brain on Earth now. Smarter and more intelligent than any machine could ever be. Someone so far removed and above everyone else on the planet that great things might now be possible. It could be a way to find the cure for all diseases, new technologies and a way to change the World for the better. But as you can imagine with that great potential and intelligence comes great fear. Fear by the Governments and fear by the many people of the World. Mankind fears what they cannot understand … or control. It is human nature in its most brutal form that is a satanic type of evil.

In nature and the wildlife kingdom animals can increase the size and strength of their herd or group and in that sense their physical powers are increased. But for man there is the technology that is the great equalizer. One man with an Uzi machine gun can defeat an army of men with spears. Yet when it comes to intelligence these laws of nature do not pass the test. In fact … they fail miserably. Ten intelligent people in a room cannot surpass the intelligence of one person that has incredible intelligence. Ten people playing chess cannot defeat a true chess master … nor can a thousand … nor can a few billion surpass the kind of intelligence that is now walking the planet we all inhabit.

When the myth started to be realized as more fact than fiction some believed the Child might be an alien sent here on Earth to learn about us … to study us … to help us … or eventually conquer us. Some thought the Child was abducted by aliens and was somehow modified and that was the reason for the incredible intelligence. Some thought the Child was a freak of nature … a Child that just happened to have an incredible brain and the brain was some kind of genetic mutation. Some thought that the Child should be treasured to help solve all the World's problems. And a few thought the Child should be free and left alone. Others thought we should study the Child for the benefit of all mankind. And some thought the Child was from God … for some divine purpose here on Earth and that the Child wasn't even born, as we know it. Some thought the Child had always existed here and had decided that now was the time of the revealing. Others thought it was the beginning of the "Armageddon" referring to the bible and the end of the World.

The parents had disappeared with the Child and were now gone. Vanished it seems without a trace but no one knows where they went or where they presently are? Or more importantly where the Child is? There are no birth records for the Child. They mysteriously disappeared both in hard copy and digital form. So little seemed to be known about this Child's history? There were no pictures that anyone knew of? They too had disappeared.

But none of them had any idea on the enormity of what this particular Child could do and how this individual could change the World not just for the better but also for the worse. They had no idea what the word "Infinite" or "Omnipotent" truly meant. And the Child's intelligence and abilities were growing ... daily. The intelligence was increasing at an exponential rate.

Some called the Child "The Child with God's Brain." The Government of United States became aware of this super intelligence and had a "Code Name" for the Child. It was simply "Y.S.B." Those three short letters were to become the "Code Name" known around the World. The Hunt for Y.S.B. was on. And all the Governments wanted this Child no matter what. In fact ... when the word truly spread across the planet the rewards started to grow and grow for this little Child. They wanted this Child but they were also becoming afraid. Afraid the Child would be captured by some other government ... an enemy government and exploited against them. Of course they wanted to exploit the Child's intelligence as well. That is the irony of it all. But the Child must be taken alive at all costs. There was no value if the Child was dead.

There was a huge bounty but only if the Child was captured alive. The bounty or reward for the capture was growing rapidly and would eventually reach 100 million dollars. Soon there would be many hunting for this tiny human treasure. Before long every Government in the World was searching for this little Child and her parents and they were using all their vast resources available to find the Child. But in the beginning there was not a trace of the Child. It was as if the family had disappeared off the face of the Earth. The hunt for Osama Bin Laden paled in comparison to this great manhunt or I should say "Little Child Hunt." But be careful what you wish for ... or we should say ... what you hunt for. Especially when you don't understand the nature of the Beast ... or in this case ... the Nature of the Child.

CHAPTER 2

GENESIS - ZERO TO PRE - FOUR YEARS - SNAPSHOT:

Jeremiah 1:5

"Before I formed you in the womb I knew you, and before you were born I consecrated you; I appointed you a prophet to the nations."

As far as anyone in the public or government knew, the beginnings were quiet and without incident. They were wrong though. There used to be a birthdate for the Child but now the records were gone. There is no physical record or digital record of the Child ever being born. No medical or dental records of any kind. They have all been wiped out but no one knows how? They believe the Child was born at the local hospital but that is about it.

In the beginning the urban types of legends were that the parents were two P.H.D. Professors who graduated from the prestigious Stanford University in California. The father a neurobiologist and the mother a neuroscientist worked at a facility not named. The father was an American and the mother of Chinese descent. And at first some thought that must be where the little baby got the incredibly smart brain … from the parent's intelligence. They were all wrong though. Genetics had nothing to do with it. And the parent's research at the facility did not play a factor either.

The parents had been trying for over three years to have a Child until finally it happened. And so the Child was born on the eighth day at the eighth hour and eighth second and the parents, the family, and the few friends they had were happy at the birth. She was a healthy baby girl weighing in at exactly 8 pounds, 8 ounces. They named the baby "Caitlin," after the father's adopted great grandmother who had passed some years earlier. The parents also liked the name because it meant "pure" and "unsullied." It was the parent's first baby and they were delighted it was a girl. Not that it mattered so much to them. They would have been just as happy with a baby boy. As long as it was a healthy baby that was the main thing. The family was not a large family. There seemed to be few relatives. The father had actually been adopted at a very young age. His natural parents had died tragically in some kind of terrible fire. An accident or so it seemed. He had no siblings. His adopted parents had later died in a car accident a few years before he got his P.H. D. The mother was orphaned when she was seven years old. The mother had come to America to live with relatives and to study many years ago and that is where she met Michael, who was to become her husband. As far as anyone could tell the parents were well ... nobodies. There was nothing outstanding in their histories. No anomalies. They were smart with their P.H. D.'s but they seemed to blend in nicely. Strangely ... there were very few records on the two parents as well? There were supposed to be records ... there just weren't any? They had been wiped out too?

The baby at birth seemed normal by all accounts and the Child was discharged from the hospital just one day after birth but it didn't take long for both parents to notice their new baby girl's intelligence was extraordinary. The parents were careful not to divulge anything about their little girl to anyone ... including the few family members and few friends they had. It was the great secret. It had to be. They realized that within the very first week. That there had to be a great secret kept from the World at all costs. No one could know. Too much was at risk. It must be done.

The parents were very protective of their new baby girl. The little girl's intelligence surpassed her physical development and was first noticed on the seventh day after birth. There was always this look in the baby's eyes before that of being ... well ... aware ... of knowing ... of seemingly sizing things up ... analyzing things ... observing her surroundings and all interactions. She had the look of a "Thinker" if one can put it that way ... even right after her birth. And although I say her physical developments lagged behind the intellectual ... her physical development was not normal either. In fact, the physical abilities of motor control and development were eons ahead of what Child Development experts would expect.

All babies take a few months ... usually 9 to 12 months or so before starting to make baby speech like sounds and mimicking human speech as they learn and decipher sounds and patterns in language. There was none of that with this particular baby though. It was on the seventh day after birth that the little girl began to speak. It wasn't a "Goo Goo or Gaah Gaah" either. It wasn't even "Mama" or "Dada" as the first word. In fact ... it wasn't sounds or even one word that came or was emitted first from this little girl's throat. It was a full sentence that was the first uttering from her tongue. Her first words were "I want to watch the Television." Now how strange is that; a seven day old baby uttering a four syllable word in a sentence let alone any single word? And yet she spoke a complete sentence with meaning. The little baby girl said it to both parents just after supper seven days after leaving the mother's womb. And the baby sat up and looked at the parents in her crib before she spoke that first sentence. She struggled sitting up … like a baby zebra at birth might struggle on the African Plains to stand minutes after birth so as to have the best chance for survival. Both father and mother were aghast! There had been no signs of anything different before this. Not really! There was a look of disbelief followed by silence as both parents stared at the baby … then at each other … then at the baby again. Then there was some shrieking by the mother … and the father. I mean that had to be not just shocking but well … a miracle?

"Did the baby just say what I think she said?" The mother asked the father.

The father stuttered as he answered, "I heard it too … but it can't be? It isn't …even possible?"

Both parents looked at their baby girl in utter shock. They were so shocked that silence filled the room for the next few seconds. It was like a dream.

Then the baby Caitlin repeated, " I want to watch the television!" She eyed both Mommy and Daddy.

More silence and then, "You … want to watch … the television?" The father stammered to his baby daughter. Both parent's eyes were wide in shock and disbelief.

Little Caitlin answered matter of fact, "Yes."

The mother who was breathing deeply managed to ask her baby, "How can you talk? It is not possible?" Then she spoke to her husband, "What the hell is going on Michael?"

Michael answered, "I have no idea and I am as stunned as you are Nuwa?"

The father obviously didn't know and the little girl said no more words. The father slowly walked over staring all the time at his daughter and then picked up little Caitlin and carried her into the living room to turn on and watch the television with his daughter. The mother followed. All three sat on the couch watching the television. The father handed the baby to the mother to hold. At first the parents tried to find a show suitable for the baby but the baby would have none of that. The baby … wanted to watch the news?

Those little eyes were watching television. Mommy and Daddy were barely looking at the TV but were rather staring at their little girl. Then the father grabbed the remote control and put on the closed caption feature. The mother looked at her husband in disbelief but then again … it kind of made sense? Silly sense but sense still the same and the baby watched the television taking it all in like a tiny sponge.

The mother then asked her infant, "How … how… I mean how much English do you know?"

The baby looked at her Mommy without blinking but didn't answer for a second. She just turned back and kept watching television.

Then the baby answered, "I'm still learning," while she still eyed the television.

The baby watched the news with her parents for about 30 minutes. The baby was making faces and seemed to be thinking about what was happening and what was being said on the television. She didn't ask any questions nor talk anymore. The parents were in total shock!

Later before bed little Caitlin directed her Mommy and Daddy, "Leave a few books in my crib! And the light on for just a bit. I want you to read to me Mommy." So Mommy read to the baby … not like any other baby now but more like teaching the baby the print. Little baby Caitlin did ask a few questions but they were more the why type of questions. She made a lot of well … thinking faces as she was read to. As far as toys go she wasn't really interested in them. There was one exception though … a rag doll. A rag doll of a little girl with black hair in pigtails and a white summertime flowered dress. She named her rag doll "Sally" and she took it everywhere with her.

At first the parents would always leave baby books in the crib as baby Caitlin wanted but it wasn't long until little Caitlin soon asked for other types of books. Books that a Child of grade 6 might read and she started walking … no crawling stage for her … at only four weeks old. By the eighth week the baby was reading high school books. By about the twelfth week little Caitlin was reading books just as fast as one could turn the pages … no matter what the content or difficulty. They were all … well … Child's play to her. She reached University level papers and books by the seventh month. The baby also began looking over, or rather studying some papers the father brought home from work. Nuwa stayed home on Maternity Leave to look after the baby and to teach the baby … or rather try to teach her daughter. It was difficult to keep up. Little Caitlin had the ability to expand her knowledge base at incredible speeds. The parents decided it would be best that Nuwa always stay with little Caitlin.

And so that is how it was in the beginning. Within two months the baby was watching the television in different languages … Spanish … French … and more all with the closed captioning on. And she learned at light speed. She only had to see or hear things once and it was in her little head. Some might label it a type of "Photographic Memory" but it was even beyond that. The baby also had an "Eidetic Memory," recalling images or sounds and well everything in her senses. By the way … the baby was developing more than the normal five senses that humans traditionally have. The parents did not know that yet. They were already afraid though. They read about some very smart people in the past with super high I.Q.'s and how many of them had difficult lives. They were well aware that their baby surpassed all those other "so-called geniuses." They wanted their Child to have a normal life but this level of intelligence would be a problem … a very big problem indeed. And they were worried about her social development. The parents made sure to teach little Caitlin ethics and morality lessons as they thought they would be especially important for her to learn. They even taught her about GOD and the many different religions and beliefs of people on the planet. The parents had to try and learn as well but it wasn't long before they couldn't keep up. The parents were right but they had no idea how important those ethics and morality lessons were for her … and mankind in the future. Little Caitlin spent much time on the computer searching the web … always looking for more to learn. You don't expect a baby or such a young Child to be sitting in front of a computer working the keyboard with proficiency when only a few weeks old.

The great secret was hidden from all until the Child was not yet four years of age. By then the baby was smarter in all areas than any adult no matter what the specialized field. And the books she was reading were books of knowledge, science, medicine, technology, computers, history, weather, environment, social problems, mechanics and such. She read very few books for entertainment or enjoyment. She read a few but it was knowledge this Child devoured and craved. She read a lot and gathered information from the Internet.

The parents had decided to have their Child take an I.Q. test but they wanted to do it quietly. But upon thinking about it they thought what would be the purpose? They already were pretty sure any I.Q. test would be … well … just a waste of time. It would be like having a radar gun with a limit of 300 miles per hour (480 kilometres per hour) trying to measure the speed of light … or even beyond the speed of light. You simply can't measure something that approaches limitless. And it would also draw attention to their little girl and that they did not want.

Little baby Caitlin's mathematic skills far surpassed that of her parents some time ago. Her skills and abilities were already solid in MSC levels one, two, and three and far beyond. She began reading and studying Einstein's Theory of Relativity and much more. The math she was studying was fast becoming rudimentary to her. It was as if her abilities were innate. Nativism versus Empiricism would be the theories that come to mind. Or could it be a combination of both or was there even more involved? Later … in a very short time she would develop her own mathematics without the use of symbols. It would be a new math but only for her. Einstein would not have understood her math. No one would. She surpassed the Quantum Mechanics of Einstein months earlier. No matter what the academic discipline … whether it was theoretical physics, astrophysics, chemistry, mathematics, including harmonic analysis, additive combinatorics, and the long list of other disciplines in today's World she had already far surpassed the smartest people on the planet in their various fields and she was not even four years old yet. In fact … she had already surpassed by far the smartest person to have ever lived. That was obvious. She was a true Polymath. And the little girl's intelligence and knowledge continued to grow and accelerate. There was no point in sending the Child to any school. She did not need a teacher or a tutor, especially since there were no teachers or tutors capable of teaching her. There would be nothing anyone could teach her now … not academically anyway … not on an intellectual level. She was self-aware in these matters and would learn and teach herself in those other areas. She needed to learn the ways of the World. The social ways … the laws … the way society was … the way the people were … the way business, medicine, and governments worked. Really the way the World worked. The way other people thought and behaved. Soon the only thing her parents could teach her was ethics, manners and such. And how to survive … especially in the beginning and that would be needed in the near future. After all she was still a Child. And so that is when the parents decided to not only move but to disappear from the face of the Earth … or try to. They needed a plan and someone to help them. It was the only way. They searched the web looking at the obituaries in many Countries. They all needed some new identities … just in case. That is how it may have started. There was much to do. Their exit plan must be perfect and leave no traces for others to follow. Or as little Caitlin would say, "There should be no footprints left in the sand that others could follow."

CHAPTER 3

THE EARLY YEARS: BEGINNING SUSPICIONS

Mathew 18:10

"See that you do not despise one of these little ones. For I tell you that in heaven their angels always see the face of my Father who is in heaven."

And so the parents began some months earlier on an exit plan. They would need multiple passports with different names, and all the extra forms of identifications all under different names. They were fairly certain they would be needed in the future. The parents even joked about it a bit although they knew it was really no laughing matter. They would have to devise a plan on when and how they would leave, where would they go, and when they got there what would they do? They had some money as they had well paying jobs and were good with their finances but here is the thing. The father had some monies from the life insurance when his parents died. Both sets of parents had life insurance. It is only rumor but it is widely believed after the fact that the baby started to look at the financial markets in the World and was giving advice to the parents on where to put their money so as to gain the greatest profits. And they were good at it … very good at it. So good in fact that it was starting to draw attention to their "so-called luck." But the family and Child were very good and seemed to be always at least one step or more ahead of anyone tracking their finances. Soon they would set up and even have investments under different names via their various identifications. And it is believed little Caitlin had much to do with the exit plan.

There are at least four known incidents that necessitated the exit plan. The first was when Caitlin was not yet four years old. It was August and Mommy was out grocery shopping in Belmont, California with Caitlin when the Child asked to meet a lady in the parking lot. The lady was obviously homeless but little Caitlin insisted on meeting her.

"Mommy … take me to that lady over there." Little Caitlin pointed towards the stranger.

"We have to be careful of strangers Caitlin. Remember what I told you about strangers?" Mommy whispered.

"Mommy ... I need to talk with her. Take me over there please." The Child really wanted to talk with the stranger.

"Oh, all right but only for a minute Caitlin. We have to get the groceries home." Mommy told her daughter.

And so the mother led her daughter over to meet with the stranger who was sitting on the curb in the parking lot.

"Excuse me ma'am but my daughter wanted to come over and meet you. I am sorry but she was quite persistent to talk with you. Do you mind?" The mother was obviously uncomfortable.

"Oh my ... why that is quite all right. You have a lovely daughter. I had a daughter once too but she is gone now." The homeless lady seemed to sigh. The lady was a sight of poverty and seemed without hope. Her tattered clothes and all that she owned she carried in her shopping cart, her face somewhat dirty and weathered.

"And what is your name you little angel?" The lady asked the Child.

"My name is Caitlin and I am sorry about your daughter and her drug overdose."

"What! But how ... how did you know about my daughter?" The stranger asked with some small tears beginning to well up in her sad, hopeless eyes.

The mother was herself in shock. This was a first. "Sometimes my daughter guesses or has a prediction." The mother quickly tried to minimize the impact of what little Caitlin had said. In reality the mother had no idea where her daughter's statement came from. It was like it was right out of left field.

Then little Caitlin held out her tiny hand to the stranger and asked, "Will you hold my hand for a minute please?"

The lady smiled and held out her left hand but the mother wasn't sure about this?

"I am not sure this is a good idea Caitlin? We should leave this lady alone now." The mother told her daughter but Caitlin would have none of that.

"It is okay Mommy. Trust me." She was looking directly at her Mommy.

The mother moved closer … just in case and her breathing increased. She was a bit nervous how this meeting was going with her young daughter.

Little Caitlin moved closer and took hold of the stranger's outstretched left hand. Caitlin looked into the homeless lady's eyes and suddenly Caitlin's other little hand reached out to touch the lady's hair and head. There was a strange silence for a few seconds and then little Caitlin said, "I want you to know that everything is going to be all right. That you are going to be okay."

"Why … thank you Child." The homeless lady responded … her eyes were wider than before as she stared at the mother but mostly at the Child.

Suddenly the mother said, "Okay Caitlin … we better be going. Say good-bye to the nice lady."

The stranger let go of Caitlin's hand with a quizzical look on her face and her only response was, "You are a very special Child. I can tell. Thank you for coming over to talk with me and meet me. Most people when they see me turn away and ignore me … like I don't exist … like I'm nothing."

Little Caitlin turned and grabbed her Mommy's hand and said, "Mommy … walk with me over there. I want to talk with you." Caitlin led her Mommy about thirty feet away.

They walked away … then stopped. "Mommy … I want to give Sarah some of our groceries that we have in the car. And how much money do you have in your purse?"

The mother was surprised. This was not something she had ever done before. She had given money and donations to the shelters but this was different. It was more personal and moving. And how did Caitlin know the lady's name was Sarah? It wasn't mentioned. And how did Caitlin know about the daughter's drug overdose?

"We can give her some food honey but we shouldn't give her any money as she might use that for drugs or something?"

"She's not on any drugs Mommy. She's never used drugs before."

"How do you know that?" The mother responded as she glanced a quick look at the homeless lady sitting on the curb.

"I just know Mommy. How much money is in your purse? I think it is $87.55?"

The mother checked and by God her daughter was right. There was $87.55 in her purse.

"That is not enough. We will give her some groceries and the $87.55 from your purse and ask the lady to wait a minute. We need to go inside the store and use the Interact machine and take out another $1,000.00 for Sarah."

The mother responded, "What! We can't give that stranger $1,000.00! Caitlin … people don't do that!"

Little Caitlin stared up at her mother in a deafening silence. The mother's face began to feel like it was turning red … not from anger … but from embarrassment.

Caitlin looked up to her Mommy and said, "We aren't regular people Mommy." Little Caitlin had some small tears beginning in her eyes.

Mommy was definitely moved by her little girl and how she thought of others less fortunate. "Okay honey but we will need to talk later. That is a lot of money to just give away."

And so little Caitlin and Mommy went to the car and put together a few bags of food for the homeless lady … took out $87.55 from the purse for the lady and walked towards the lady sitting on the curb.

"You can give it to her honey." The mother said to little Caitlin as they approached.

Little Caitlin told her Mommy, "We'll both give it to Sarah Mommy."

And so they went to the lady … gave the groceries and the $87.55 from the purse, and then asked the lady to wait for just a minute. Then Mommy and little Caitlin went to the Interact machine inside the store and took out $1,000.00 and gave it to the lady.

The homeless lady … Sarah was ecstatic and thanked both of them profusely.

Little Caitlin just said, "Remember what I said … that you are going to be okay now." Then the little girl leaned in close and whispered into Sarah's ear two words. "It's gone."

Sarah began to cry and little Caitlin gave the homeless lady a hug. As they were leaving the homeless lady called out to both of them, "God Bless you! God Bless both of you!"

The lady wasn't exactly sure what the little girl meant when she said, "It's gone." She couldn't know? The experience touched her in a way she had never known.

Once in the car and driving the mother said, "Caitlin … that was very nice of you but you can't be doing that all the time. Let's just make this a one-time thing … okay?"

Little Caitlin looked at her Mommy and said, "I cured her Mommy. I made it go away."

"What do you mean you cured her?" The mother looked over at little Caitlin in surprise.

"The sickness Mommy. I made it go away. It was on her brain and I got rid of it."

The mother was in shock yet again. She could hardly drive and so found a safe place and pulled over quickly. "What do you mean it was on her brain and you got rid of it?" She asked her daughter. Her face was in shock!

"Sarah had a tumor on her brain Mommy. It would have killed her in about four months. She knows that. I got rid of it … or rather most of it. It will all be gone within three days."

"How … do you know … she has a tumor Caitlin?" The mother was in total shock!

"I saw it Mommy. Or rather I kind of saw it … hard to explain? She'll be fine now though."

The mother began to cry as they both sat in the car on the roadside.

"It's okay Mommy. Don't cry. It'll be okay. I'll take care of you." Little Caitlin gave her Mommy a big hug.

After about ten minutes mother was kind of okay to drive and so they drove home. First though they had to stop to replace those groceries they gave away to Sarah. They used a credit card this time. Once home the mother talked with little Caitlin some more about what had happened. Little Caitlin didn't tell her Mommy all of it though. It would be better to wait before telling her parents just what she could do. That evening when the father returned home Nuwa told him what had happened at the grocery store parking lot with the homeless lady. And so the father and mother went in the kitchen to talk with their very special little girl. They made some hot chocolate … with seven of those colored mini-marshmallows in each cup.

"I think it would be a good idea to start to think about developing a plan to leave very soon … just in case we have to leave the area quickly. And we have to teach you Caitlin to be more careful how you talk to strangers. Mentioning the homeless lady's daughter and drug overdose will draw unwanted attention. Or knowing people's names when they don't even tell you. Curing that lady of the tumor … well … I don't even know how to respond to that?" The mother agreed and so stage one of an exit plan began to develop.

"The lady's name was Sarah Daddy," little Caitlin added, "and she's going to be all right now!!!"

Daddy and Mommy just stared at their little girl wondering … wondering if it could be true?

The second incident happened on an evening two months later in October. Little Caitlin, mother, and father had just finished supper Monday night when Caitlin suddenly mentioned out of the blue about a plane crash.

"Mommy … Daddy … there is going to be a plane crash tomorrow morning and we should warn them." Caitlin just blurted out as they all sat in the living room.

"What do you mean there's going to be a plane crash Caitlin? Do you mean you saw one on the television? Is that what you meant?" Father asked.

"No … the plane will crash Tuesday morning leaving New York at 9:19 A.M. just after takeoff. It is flight 1536 bound for Cancun. There will be 260 people on board and all will die." Caitlin told her parents.

"How do you know that Caitlin?" Father asked with eyes wide open in disbelief.

"I just know it Daddy. I don't exactly know how? I just do. It will be an engine failure on the right side that causes the crash. We need to warn them."

"Even if you are right and we warn them that will draw major attention to us and that is not good." The mother answered as she looked at her husband.

"Are you sure about this Caitlin? Are you really sure this will happen?" The mother asked little Caitlin.

Little Caitlin nodded her head yes. And she understood the danger it would draw to her if it was reported but to little Caitlin it had to be done. Most would think it was a terrorist attack and that the family was somehow connected to the crash. Or if the public believed their daughter could predict the future that would be a huge problem as well.

In the end the parents decided to do nothing. Not to call and warn the airline or the various news agencies. Their daughter might be wrong after all but in reality the parents weren't so sure. They were at the point when nothing their daughter could do surprised them. Or that is what they thought but they would soon discover they could indeed be surprised even more by this little girl.

"Mommy … Daddy … those people are all going to die if we don't help them. We can stop it."

Both parents looked at their little girl with anguish on their faces.

"Oh Michael … is there nothing we can do … all those people … they have families … and the Children?" Nuwa asked. She knew in her heart what must be done though. Nothing!

Michael answered, "If only there was some way we could be sure they wouldn't be able to track us. And likely they wouldn't even believe us if we did try to tell them. No … we must not do anything and hope we are making the right decision."

Little Caitlin made a face at Mommy and Daddy and her little heart was sad … sad for all the people who would now have no chance to live. It would be a long night.

There was anxiety in the family that morning hoping that nothing would happen. Little Caitlin was persistent though that the plane crash was imminent. The father decided to stay home and phoned in sick so he could work at home …

and watch the television. The parents sat listening to the news … hoping nothing would happen … hoping their daughter was wrong. Then at 9:32 A.M. CNN broke the news about a plane crash in New York. Flight 1536 had crashed just after takeoff. The parents were still shocked and felt terrible. The news reported they expected it unlikely there would be any survivors.

"Oh Michael … we should have at least tried … all those people." The teary eyed mother managed to say between sobs. Michael was quiet. He didn't know what to say?

"Those stupid, stupid people! They didn't do anything!" Caitlin blurted out and she looked angry as she watched the television. "How dumb are they?"

The father and mother turned to look at their little girl. The father asked his little girl, "What do you mean they didn't do anything Caitlin?"

Daddy and Mommy waited for a response. It seemed like all the air had left the room and their hearts were pounding even more. Little Caitlin looked at her parents and she knew their hearts were pounding stronger now. She could feel it.

"I phoned the airline and told them that plane would crash. I told them the time … the flights number … the number of people on board. And I told them it was not a terrorist attack but would be a mechanical failure. They asked my name and I hung up." Caitlin told Mommy and Daddy.

"You called? Caitlin … you called them? You called them from here? What time did you call? What did they say Caitlin?" The mother asked.

"I called the airline at 4:00 A.M. and I called them from here. I know they can trace it but I … made sure they are going to have a lot of trouble doing that. They wanted to know my name. That is when I hung up." Little Caitlin declared.

Then the father spoke. "You called and warned them and it didn't make any difference. Now they will be coming here to talk with us. Exactly what we don't want or need. What are we going to do?"

Caitlin assured her father, "They will try to find us but I took care of that. Don't worry Mommy and Daddy. It will take a long time for them to figure out where the call came from. At least till the end of June. I made sure of that."

"How did you do that Caitlin?" The mother asked. Both mother and father were extremely worried and the little Child tried to reassure them.

Caitlin looked at them for a few seconds and then told them, "You won't understand how but I can control their technology and communication networks … at least most of them. It is going to be on the news about the phone call but it will be a mystery until the end of June … June 30th to be exact."

The parents were quite shocked as you can imagine. Caitlin kept reassuring them as best she could.

The mother looked at her daughter and asked the question that needed to be asked. "Can you tell the future Caitlin?" The father and mother waited for the answer with baited breath.

Little Caitlin looked directly into her parents eyes and said, "In a sense sometimes I can. I am still learning and developing. The future can be changed though, sometimes by the simplest of things. That is the beauty of it. Don't ask me about the future just yet Mommy and Daddy. All I ask is that you trust me. We should get ready to move though. We should be ready to move earlier in June. That still leaves us some time. I love you Mommy and Daddy."

And so the family began to plan for a June exit. It was time to leave the Country and get lost somewhere on the planet Earth. The parents started searching discreetly on how to become lost. Lost in the World so no one could find them. They knew that when news broke they would have to remain hidden … that they would be on the run in a World that would suddenly seem not so large. The Child believed that also after reading so much and understanding the true nature of the Governments … and man. The parents would have to study and learn of any travel restrictions for the different Countries in the World. The passport travel Visas, what were the currency restrictions for entry and exit, vaccinations, and what needed to be declared? They wanted the travel to be seamless without any questions. They made sure they had return tickets but realized that they would not be using those return tickets. The return tickets would act as a decoy or a smoke screen. But before that time there would be two more incidents of importance.

CHAPTER 4

GOVERNMENT INTEREST: GETTING READY

Proverbs 20:17

"Bread gained by deceit is sweet to a man, but afterward his mouth will be full of gravel."

The third incident happened in mid May. It was a visit from the United States Security and Exchange Commission. It seemed the family's success with their investments in stocks and funds had garnished some interest by certain departments in the government. There was starting to be a belief that the family's financial successes were beyond just pure luck. All their investments and their trades were … well … exceptional in that profits were maximized beyond regular norms. It was little Caitlin who broke the news about a week before it happened. It was a Saturday morning at the breakfast table when Caitlin told them.

"Mommy … Daddy … I need to warn you about something." Instantly the parents had a worried look on their faces. "I don't want you to worry and that is why I am telling you this now … ahead of time. There will be some government men coming here to the house on Friday to ask questions about your investments. They have been investigating your holdings for a few months … monitoring your trades and they think something is not right. They think you may be getting some kind of insider tips. I am telling you this so you will be prepared and not be shocked. You will have to act shocked though when the government men come." Little Caitlin emphasized, "You are only to answer their questions and not offer any other information. This is important." Caitlin was starting to sound like an experienced lawyer. In reality she was smarter by far than any lawyer or investigator. "And don't go downtown with them. Ask them to come in. Be friendly and they are going to try and separate both of you so they can talk to you individually. Keep me in the room with both of you. I will find a way to get in your ear if there are any doubts."

"Should we be worried Caitlin? We haven't broken any laws but that doesn't stop the government sometimes." The father asked his daughter who had just turned four years old a few months earlier.

"Try not to worry Mommy and Daddy. The government is just on a … how do you say it … quite strange really … but they are on nothing but a fishing trip … or a wild goose hunt."

And so through the week little Caitlin prepped the parents on everything about the visit so that by Friday they seemed much more at ease when thinking about the upcoming visit. Their faith in their special Child had much to do with that.

At 10:00 A.M. sharp there was a loud knock on the door and little Caitlin and Daddy walked to the door and opened it to see two men in suits. The mother remained in the living room.

"May I help you?" The father asked the suits.

"Are you Mr. Brennan? … A Mr. Michael Brennan?" One of the suits asked.

"Yes … I am Michael Brennan … and who are you?

"I am Mr. Williams and this is Mr. Wood. We are with the United States Security and Exchange Commission. We would like to talk with you and your wife about some of your investments Mr. Brennan. Is your wife home?" Suit number one said.

"Yes … she is home. What is it exactly you want to talk about Mr. Williams?" The father asked.

"Well … we would like you and your wife to come downtown to our local office where we could talk Sir." Mr. Williams was doing all the talking. The other suit was quiet and watching. "Could you find someone to look after your daughter? Or perhaps we could set up a time for you and your wife to come to our office?"

"No … we can't and won't go downtown to talk but I will invite you both to come in so we can answer any questions you may have. It is quite strange to have the Commission at our door you understand?" The father replied.

The two suits looked at each other ... nodded and the other suit said, "Thank you Sir. We will come in. I hope we can clear all this up quickly."

"I hope so too!" replied the father. "This is my daughter Caitlin."

And so the two suits came in and were introduced to the mother who was sitting in the living room. They all sat in the living room ... including little Caitlin.

"Sorry to bother you but we have some questions about your investment activities and your portfolio investments. It is standard procedure when some people's investments are doing much better than expected. I wonder if Mr. Wood could talk with Mrs. Brennan separately somewhere and perhaps your daughter could play somewhere else?" Mr. Williams requested.

This time the mother answered, "No ... you can talk with both of us here and my daughter stays! She has a special condition and I want her to be near us." The two suits had no idea just what "special" meant in this case. "My husband takes care of most of the investments anyway but he does talk about them with me."

"Very well." Mr. Williams answered. For these two government suits people were always guilty first and had to prove their innocence. They were both experienced investigators.

"I must tell you that there have been some flags raised the last few months on your stock trading and investments. When things start to seem too successful it is flagged at our department to first monitor and then investigate. And your investments have done exceptionally well the last while. That is why we need to meet and talk with both of you." Mr. Williams said.

Both suits were looking for any signs of uneasiness in the parents. Their experience was that most people who were guilty showed it in their demeanor or when they tried to answer questions. There was none of that here though.

The parents answered the questions matter of fact and the father just stated he had been extremely fortunate the last few months and it was really a combination of some financial skill but mostly just luck. The questions lasted an hour and in the end the suits left. They were not totally satisfied though. They would continue monitoring the family's investments and both suits were sure there would be a second visit.

After the suits left the house the father said to his wife and his little girl, "We are scheduled to leave in June. Do we need to exit earlier? What do you think?"

Really the question was for little Caitlin. Caitlin replied, "No … we don't need to leave early. When we leave though we will leave for good. I will guide you on what must be done."

"Perhaps we should change our investments so we lose some money. Maybe that will make them less suspicious?" The father asked.

Little Caitlin's answer to that was, "No … it won't make any difference. They will still suspect us and would just think we are trying to trick them by losing money. We are only a little over a month from leaving and we will be safe from these government men." And so they all decided to stick to their original plan.

Then the fourth incident happened in early June. Little Caitlin told the parents what was to happen. This time though it was the interests of the National Security Agency, or the N.S.A. that was drawn to the family. Little Caitlin told her parents about the National Security Agency and that they had an interest in the family for the last month. The heat was beginning to build.

"I need to tell you something Mommy and Daddy." Little Caitlin made sure they were already seated.

Both parents looked at their little girl and thought, "Oh my … what is it now?" And they were right to think so.

"You are being investigated by the National Security Agency and it is my fault but we are okay."

"Why are we being investigated by the National Security Agency and how is it your fault? What did you do?" The father asked in dread. The little girl certainly had her parent's attention.

"Well … I have been researching the defense and communication systems of the United States Government. The M.D.S. or Missile Defense System … some offensive systems … special communications like satellite capabilities, and some other areas."

The Mommy asked, "Why would you want to know about those things Caitlin? Why are they of interest to you?"

"I'll need that information in the future … even though capabilities can change. They are important when we leave … to stay hidden and safe. Right now the phone is wire tapped … since this morning. They are going to visit us in a couple of days but you will obviously act very surprised. They are coming Thursday. When they ask their questions I will say it was I and that I was just curious about it for some reason. That I have an interest in things and that you had no idea I was looking at such things. They will believe me. At least at first and by that time we will be gone."

"Holy crap!" The father managed to blurt out.

Then the mother let slip, "Oh shit!" she quickly added, "Oops," when she realized she swore in front of her daughter. She turned to look at her daughter.

Little Caitlin quickly said, "Hey Mommy … no swearing! It will be okay. They are going to be satisfied with our answers. The visit will only be for 45 minutes."

The father and mother were … well … even more in shock than the previous visit by the United States Security and Exchange Commission just a few weeks earlier. I mean these things just don't happen to most people!

"It will be a breeze. Just let me do some of the talking. You just say you had no idea I was surfing the web for such information and that you will definitely be monitoring me … your daughter much more closely from now on. The N.S.A. man and woman are actually going to have a little laugh about it."

"I love you Mommy. I love you Daddy." Little Caitlin said it so cutely. Both parents just sighed and said together, "We love you too Caitlin."

Then the father added, "I think I am going to have a heart attack?"

Little Caitlin looked at her Daddy … smiled and said, "You aren't going to have a heart attack Daddy. Don't be such a drama queen."

The mother was surprised at that remark then burst out laughing. Soon they were all laughing with tears in their eyes. They all laughed and laughed. The little girl was certainly full of surprises.

Two days later a man and a woman were knocking at the front door and waited for someone to answer. Little Caitlin answered the door with her mother this time.

"Why hello little girl. Oh hello." The man at the door said when he noticed the mother behind the little girl. "Are you Mrs. Brennan?"

"Yes I am and who are you?" The mother had a look of surprise on her face. It was worthy of an Academy Award although she was still really surprised that the N.S.A. agents were at her door.

"We are from the National Security Agency or the N.S.A. I am Agent Baxter and this is my associate Agent White." The female stated. Both Agents flashed their badges. That wasn't their real names. "Is Mr. Brennan here? We would like to talk with both of you."

"Yes … my husband is here. I will get him. This is our daughter Caitlin."

"Why hello Caitlin." Agent Baxter then asked, "And how old are you?"

Little Caitlin smiled slightly and answered, "I am four and a half."

"What is this about?" The mother asked the two N.S.A. agents at the door. They just asked if they could come in for a few minutes to talk. Mother then invited the two agents inside the house to the living room.

"If we could talk with your husband as well we could let you know what this is about." Agent White now spoke.

Mommy then called out, "Michael!! Come here please!"

The father walked into the living room where everyone was and when told who the visitors were he too acted surprised. They had their introductions and then they all sat down.

"The reason we are here Mr. and Mrs. Brennan is that we have noticed some very unusual activity on your computer. Do you have any idea what that might be?"

Both parents answered, "No … we have no idea? What is it?"

There was a pause and then Agent Baxter said, "Well … it has come to our attention that a computer at this address has been accessing information regarding defense systems, communication systems, and the nuclear capabilities of the United States of America."

"Whaaat? Are you sure?" The mother wasn't acting here. She had no idea about the nuclear stuff.

The father quickly added, "That can't be? You must be mistaken?" The father had that same look of shock. Little Caitlin had never mentioned anything to the parents that she was looking into nuclear information.

The N.S.A. agents were gauging the response of the parents. "Is there perhaps someone else with access to the computer?"

Both parents turned to look at little Caitlin who had a look on her face of a little puppy dog that just pooped on the rug. That little girl could act also it seemed.

"That was me Mommy and Daddy. I was interested in all that stuff after watching the news. Did I do something bad?" Little Caitlin used her winning Oscar voice.

Both agents looked at the little girl and then Agent Baxter asked, "You were on the computer looking that stuff up?"

Little Caitlin answered, "Yes … I am interested in all that stuff. Even though I don't understand it I still find it real cool."

Both the agents sat back in the chairs with a puzzled look on their faces. It was obvious they were trying to determine if this could be true.

Then the mother added, "Our little girl is a special little girl. She is very smart for her age and so really has an interest in … a lot of different things."

"And she is quite a handful at times as you can imagine. She is a great little girl but she does keep us on our toes. We are going to have to have a long talk with her and monitor her computer time much more closely." The father added to the agents. "We do have a P-O-R-N blocker on the computer so she doesn't know about S-E-X until we are ready." The father spelled out those words.

Then little Caitlin blurted out, "I know what S-E-X is but that's ugly. Not interested in that junk. What that's P-O-R thingy?"

Their little daughter knows about S-E-X? Or so she said? Everyone in the room was shocked … none more so than the parents?

"What do you mean you know about S-E-X?" The mother asked.

"That's where babies come from. Something about some stupid bird dropping off babies … right?

Both agents were trying not to laugh … or even smile.

"I am sorry. We are going to have to a very big talk with our little girl." The father said looking at the agents. Both parents acted embarrassed and in reality they were very embarrassed.

"Am I am trouble Mommy and Daddy?" Caitlin asked. "I'm sorry."

"That's okay honey. You didn't mean to cause any trouble." The mother answered.

"Well … I think we are done here. Don't you think we are done Agent Baxter?" Agent White declared.

"Yes … I think we are done. Thank you so much and we will be leaving now. Please do have a talk with your daughter. This has been cleared up quite nicely though. If you could walk us to the door." Agent Baxter asked the parents.

And so the two N.S.A. agents left. Once outside and in the car they broke down and laughed. Then Agent Baxter said, "None the less ... let's get a search warrant and check that computer?"

"Do you think that is necessary Lynne?"

"Well ... perhaps not but at least we will cover all the bases and make sure." Agent Baxter replied. "We will keep the wire taps on too!"

The other agent nodded his head in agreement. "We will get the search warrant."

"There's one other consideration that we need to be aware of." Agent Baxter added.

"And what is that?" Agent White asked.

"They have that trip booked to Berlin at the end of June ... June 28th to be exact,"

"Now that is interesting isn't it? But it could be nothing but a coincidence. Still we will have the search warrant well before that. Let's target the 10th of June." Mr. White announced.

Inside the house they all felt much more at ease after the meeting but both Mommy and Daddy wanted to know what their little daughter knew about S-E-X.

The mother asked little Caitlin, "So ... just what do you know about S-E-X young lady?"

Both parents waited with anticipation for their daughter's response.

Little Caitlin responded, "What do you want to know Mommy? I'll tell you."

The parents looked at each other in surprise. Then the father made a face at his wife … and asked her, "You only wanted the one kid … right?"

Both parents burst out laughing and they couldn't stop for about five minutes.

"Hey … what is so funny?" Little Caitlin wanted to know.

Mommy told little Caitlin, "Well … Daddy and I really wanted three kids before you came."

"I still don't get it!" Little Caitlin declared. "What's so funny?"

CHAPTER 5

THE HUNT BEGINS: HIDING

Revelation 12:14

"But the woman was given the two wings of the great eagle so that she might fly from the serpent into the wilderness, to the place where she is to be nourished for a time, and times, and half a time, out of the serpent's reach."

38

The parents began almost immediately on final plans for their exit. They were fairly prepared but were finishing up the final stages. It needed to be perfect. Little Caitlin had one more thing that she needed to tell Mommy and Daddy.

"We need to leave early Mommy and Daddy." Little Caitlin told her parents later that night.

"Why do we have to leave earlier Caitlin?" The father asked.

"The government is aware of our flight on June 28th. They are going to get a search warrant before we leave. They don't think we are guilty of anything but they are just making sure. As for the computer I have … well … modified it a bit. It is encrypted with several cloaking devices. That means they can break the first code with some work but the real data is encrypted much more securely. We should leave the computer here at the house. We don't want to take a chance it might get inspected at the airport by security. They won't like that they can't get into the computer. I never save anything on the computer because I don't need to since I can just remember everything. We can buy another computer later when we are abroad. Once the N.S.A. agents really do suspect us our flight and travel would be … restricted." Caitlin informed her parents.

"I better re-book those tickets for an earlier flight then." The father said and the mother agreed.

"No … don't do that Daddy. That will send an alert to them and make it worse. Leave those tickets and they will think nothing has changed. Those tickets were purchased at the San Francisco Airport. Right now we are considered a low risk. We should buy another set of tickets for June 7th to Berlin. We will fly out of the San Jose Airport this time. I will get you the time and flight and we will do it from the local library computer. Mommy can take me there. We can still use our real identities for now. We will be fine. We won't be staying very long in Berlin though." Little Caitlin was only telling her parents some details though. There would be more information to follow … when the parents needed to know things.

When Caitlin was in bed father and mother talked at the kitchen table as they were drinking herbal green tea.

"Well darling … I guess our lives are about to change and never be the same? How do you feel about this?" The father queried.

"Nervous for sure but we must protect her at all costs … no matter what. I do have this feeling though Michael that it won't be long before our little girl is looking after and protecting us."

"I have that same feeling. She is doing it right now when you think about it. This certainly is a different type of parenthood than we expected isn't it? Father looked lovingly at his beloved wife.

The mother nodded and then both of them noticed little Caitlin at the doorway listening to them and it startled them a bit.

"Hey darling … you're up? Trouble sleeping?" The father asked his young daughter.

"I heard you talking Mommy and Daddy. You don't have to worry. I will make everything all right. I have some more things to tell you."

Father looked at mother and just said, "Oh God! There's more?" The parents suddenly looked panicked.

Little Caitlin walked to the table and sat down in the chair between Mommy and Daddy. "It's okay Mommy and Daddy. No more trouble but I want you to be aware of some things so you don't freak out."

The parents stared in silence dreading and not knowing what she was going to talk about now.

Little Caitlin continued, "I can't tell all the future ... or rather all the things that could happen but I am learning more and more about it. I have some other abilities that other ... well ... people don't have that you are not aware of." Caitlin looked at her mother and father judging their responses.

"Okay ... what other abilities do you have Caitlin?" The Mommy asked.

"Would you get me a glass of water for me Daddy?" The father quickly got the glass of water and put it on the table in front of Caitlin. "Watch the water Mommy and Daddy."

The parents watched the glass and mother noticed little Caitlin wasn't even looking at the glass but looking at her.

"Look at the glass Mommy and see what happens." Suddenly within seconds the water was starting to freeze. Within 10 seconds the glass cracked and the water was frozen completely solid.

"Keep watching the ice." Little Caitlin told her parents.

Within seconds the ice in the cup suddenly starting to melt. Seconds later the ice was steaming and then boiling and bubbling. The glass totally broke and the water was now on the table bubbling hot. Soon nothing but a little bit of steam was on the table and then nothing.

Father and mother looked at their little daughter sitting there and then Mommy asked, "How did you do that Caitlin?" She gulped as she said it. Father just had his mouth open.

"I just thought about making the molecules moving very fast to heat it. That is the simply explanation. It has to do with energy dispersal. Heating it similar to a microwave but much more effective. I don't use waves though. The rapid cooling is the reverse effect."

"How long have you been able to do that Caitlin?" Daddy asked.

"I found out I could do it about six months ago. I even tried it out on the bathtub full of water and it doesn't take long at all. I stopped though cause I didn't want to break the tub."

"Well … I guess if we ever need ice or hot tea and the power went off we know where to come." The father said trying to smile about it as best he could.

"It could also be a weapon Daddy." Caitlin stated matter of fact.

"What do you mean a weapon Caitlin?" Mommy asked with a look on her face of wonder and concern … and fear.

"Well … the human body is mostly made of liquid and …" But Caitlin didn't get to finish.

"Caitlin! You wouldn't! Promise me that will never happen!" Mother cried out.

Then father added, "Caitlin! That would be wrong!"

"I know and I promise I won't use it to kill anyone but you must know we are going to have enemies. Enemies that will want to get me at all costs. And that includes getting to me through you. I won't permit anything to happen to either of you … no matter what."

Then Caitlin changed the subject. "I want to show you something else I can do." In secret little Caitlin was only showing her Mommy and Daddy some of the special abilities she could do at the present time. Her abilities were changing though.

"What else can you do?" Both parents happened to ask at the same time.

"I can move things with my mind. For instance … watch." Caitlin looked around in the kitchen for something to move. "Watch your mug Mommy." And the mug began to slide across the table. "Yours too Daddy." And then both mugs were sliding across the table … slowly. It was as if the mugs were dancing on a stage. "It's called Telekinesis … although mine is not a trick." Then Caitlin added, "So you want to know how much I can move don't you?"

"How much can you move Caitlin?" The father asked.

"Quite a bit actually. I am getting better at it too! I could lift you up Daddy if you want to see?" Little Caitlin kind of smiled as she said it.

"No … no … don't lift Daddy up Caitlin." The mother answered. "But how much can you lift? Do you know?"

"No … I haven't really tried yet but I did lift the sofa when you weren't in the room just to see if I could … and a parked car outside." Caitlin told her parents. "Without physically touching them."

The parents were dumbfounded and little Caitlin wondered if she told them too much at once. It was a good thing she didn't tell them about all the other stuff she could do.

Father asked, "A parked car? You can lift a parked car?

"Yea … I can." Caitlin got up to leave and said, "It's getting late. I'm going to bed. I love you Mommy and Daddy." And then she rushed to give Mommy and Daddy a big hug. As she was leaving the room she said, "Good-night Mommy and Daddy."

Mommy and Daddy said goodnight and then Daddy added, "I'll walk you to your bedroom."

And so the father walked little Caitlin to her bedroom and tucked her in and gave his little Princess a kiss. "Well … you certainly gave us quite the show tonight darling." Daddy said right after the kiss.

"I know Daddy but I do want you to know things but there is one thing I want you to tell Mommy yourself." Caitlin was whispering in her Daddy's ear.

"What's that honey?"

"That I love you both so much. That I know the sacrifices you both are making for me. That I will take care of you and especially that everything is going to be all right. That is what I want you to tell her."

Father smiled and said, "I will tell her that. We both love you so much too Caitlin. You go to sleep now."

As father was leaving the room little Caitlin called out, "Don't let the bed bugs bite Daddy." Daddy smiled … turned off the main light and the night-light came on. Little Caitlyn and Sally … her rag doll curled up in the bed ready for sleep.

When Michael got back to the kitchen Nuwa was still sitting there. She had cleaned up the broken glass off the table. She still had a look of disbelief and shock on her face. Actually both father and mother did. It was yet another revelation on the special abilities of their little girl.

Father sat down at the table and took a drink of his still hot tea. He looked at the mug and mother said, "Your daughter warmed it up for you when you were upstairs. I saw it suddenly start to bubble just a bit."

The father's only response was a very soft whispered, "Wow," and then he took a deep, deep breath.

Then mother stated in a very soft whisper, "Michael … I'm a bit worried when she said that boiling … or freezing could be used as a weapon."

"I know but we have taught her ethics and compassion and really she is a good girl."

"But she is only four years old and so much power. Do you think her powers will continue to grow?"

"I don't know but it sure looks that way. For now her powers are growing fast. She said something upstairs that she wanted you to know." The father said as he looked at his wife.

"What did she say?"

"That she loves us both very much … that we shouldn't worry too much and that she appreciates the sacrifices we both are making for her and that everything will be all right. That is what she wanted you to know."

Nuwa began to cry and Michael went over and he gave her a reassuring hug and kissed her forehead. Then he kissed her face several times.

"I love her so much Michael but I am worried about her future."

"I know … I know … I love her so much too darling." The father also had some tears in his eyes. "I think we will feel better when we have left the United States and go into hiding."

The next few days were fairly uneventful. That is when Mommy and Caitlin went to the local library to use one of the public computers to buy the airline tickets. Caitlin didn't want to use her own computer because the N.S.A. was tracking her I.P address. She knew that. Their bags were already packed and they were ready. Three tickets were purchased for a non-stop flight to Berlin. Little Caitlin even thought of a "Code Word" should there be an emergency and change of plans for leaving that they could use if need be. The "Code Word" would be "Starlight." No one would suspect. Departure would be 12:00 A.M.

The next night little Caitlin was on the computer working on some extremely complicated math formulas when she suddenly had a feeling and noticed something. The web cam was on and someone was watching her. She clicked a few keys to reverse and see a picture of just who was watching her. Normally this wouldn't have worked so easily but let's not forget this was no ordinary girl. She was more computer savvy than anyone on the planet and when she clicked she saw just who was tracking her. It was that Agent Baxter and another unknown man from the N.S.A. It was only a second but then little Caitlin terminated the connection. Caitlin pressed seven keys to start her own program. "Mommy! Daddy! … We are leaving right now! Let's go!"

CHAPTER 6

THE HUNT INTENSIFIES: THE CHASE

Luke 21:25

"And there will be signs in the sun and moon and stars, and on the earth distress of nations in perplexity because of the roaring of the sea and the wave,"

At a secret high tech surveillance room at an undisclosed location of the National Security Agency there was shock. Agent Baxter and a Senior I.T. Agent had witnessed first hand what that little girl was doing. Little Caitlin was wearing a big hat so much of her face was hidden but there was no doubt about it. It was with certainty that it was she who was doing the work. They didn't understand the formulas but recognized it as some kind of very advanced mathematical formulations and this four-year-old girl was responsible. They were both in shock.

"Did you see what I just saw?" Agent Baxter asked staring at the I. T Agent in utter shock and disbelief.

"Ah … yes … I saw it with my own eyes. Is that even possible? I don't understand these formulas at all? Do you know what they mean?" The I.T. expert asked.

Then Agent Baxter added, "That little girl was doing it? I have no clue about this math and it is beyond my abilities?" And how did she know we were watching her? You were on Stealth Mode were you not?"

"Yes … I was on Stealth and I don't know how she figured that out? I don't believe that has ever happened before? It is a new secret technology. We need to get someone here fast who can figure out these mathematic formulas?"

Within twenty minutes there were three Agents … two men and one woman in the room going over … or rather trying to go over the little girl's mathematical formulas. They couldn't. They were lost in the complexity.

The Head Agent of the group asked, "You say a little girl is responsible for this?"

"Yes Sir." The I.T Agent replied. Agent Baxter nodded in agreement.

The three so-called N.S.A. experts in Math looked at each other ... shook their heads and the Head Agent simply said, "This is bloody amazing." Then he gave the order to one of the three. "Call Agent Phoenix in right now! Send a car to his place! I want him here ten minutes ago! Do you understand! Now!"

"Yes Sir! Right away!" was the reply from one of the other so-called mathematician experts.

The Head Agent said, "I must tell you this is some high level mathematics. I don't understand much of it but what I do know is I haven't seen anything like this before. Simply bloody amazing! My God!"

"And notify all the heads right now! I want them here. Tell them it is a National Security Issue. And send a team to pick the family up right now! I want a team at their door and bring them in. How long before they can be picked up?"

"Well ... we can be at the house in 35 minutes Sir."

"Not good enough! Contact the police in the meantime and order them to get a couple of cars to the house. They are to sit outside and make sure no one leaves. Now!" The boss yelled, "Someone get me a secure line!" Another agent ran to him with a secure line. The boss punched the numbers into the phone and waited as the phone rang at the other end. After the third ring someone answered the call.

"Hello Sir ... sorry to wake you but this is Agent Black. We have a situation here and I think you need to come in Sir. Let me correct that. You need to come in Sir. No ... it can't wait till morning Sir. We've had a breach of security and I believe it has to do with our satellites and launch capabilities. We're still checking. Thank you Sir. Yes Sir." The boss hung up. "Is Agent Phoenix on his way yet?"

"Soon Sir." The female N.S.A. agent answered. "We've dispatched a vehicle to get him and we will be there shortly."

"My God! Simply amazing!" He said as he stared at the screen. "How is this even possible? Get me that girl!"

Within six minutes there were four squad cars strategically parked near the house. They sat in their cruisers waiting as instructed.

"Any idea what this is about?" One of the officers asked his Sergeant in one of the cruisers.

"No idea but my guess is it is big. We are to secure the premise and make sure no one leaves and wait for the N.S.A. people to show up. I was told they would be here within half an hour."

Twenty-nine minutes later five dark sedans showed up with Government issued plates. One man dressed in dark approached the cruiser that was in front of the house and the Sergeant powered down his window.

"Good evening Sergeant. I am Agent Orr. Has anyone entered or left the house?"

"No Sir. No one has entered or left since our arrival." The Sergeant answered.

"Thank you Sergeant. We'll take it from here." The dark suit added, "We're going to be entering the premise now if you would relay that to your men. If you and your men could continue guarding the perimeters that would be appreciated."

"Wilco that." The Sergeant responded and then relayed the message to his team.

Within seconds a number of black suits exited the sedans and instantly surrounded the house front, back and side. Three of the dark suits were at the front door and one suit knocked on the door very loudly. No answer. He knocked again and rang the doorbell. All was quiet inside the house. A couple of lights were on inside the house. The scene was quiet as the agents listened for any noise.

Four very loud knocks on the door again and the Agent yelled, "We are with law enforcement. You need to come to the door right now!"

The Agents at the door pulled out their guns and each officer was given a reminder. "Remember … under no circumstances is there to be shooting around the little girl. Roger that back."

Each Agent confirmed the instructions. Most were not expecting gunfire but you always have to be ready for it. The front door and back door was kicked in at the same time and a rush of agents crashed inside the house shouting and securing the premises with guns drawn. After a thorough search of the house it was confirmed the house was not occupied. The garage was checked and it was reported that there was no vehicle in the garage.

Agent Orr called it in to his supervisors. "Sir … we have secured the house but no one is here and there are no vehicles on the property. Yes Sir … I understand. Eyes and ears in and around the house and a clean sweep … yes Sir."

The N.S.A. already had the vehicle information and connected with Police Services to be on the lookout for a new silver Toyota Camry with license plate numbers 7FJB425. The suspects were two adults, a man and a woman, and a young Child about four years old. The mother was of Chinese descent and the little girl mixed. They were to be located and apprehended and detained until National Security Agents arrived.

A team of special agents scoured the house for clues as to the suspect's possible whereabouts or their habits. What the agents discovered as very strange was that they couldn't find any pictures … recent or past of the father and mother … nor the Child. And even more strange was that they didn't find one set of fingerprints. Even the D.M.V. information had been wiped from the system when they checked for a picture. There were no driver license records with pictures of the parents. Everything else was there but no pictures.

Airports, train stations, bus stations, and any possible mode of escape were under surveillance and not left to chance. N.S.A. and law enforcement made sure of that.

Back at N.S.A. Headquarters Agent Baxter reported to her supervisors that the family had booked a flight from the San Francisco Airport to Berlin Germany that was scheduled to leave at the end of the month. The family had return tickets.

"Check to see if they re-scheduled their flight plans. Judging by what happened earlier tonight I think the family is on the run. We can be fairly sure of that and we can't let them leave the Country." The Head Agent ordered. "Right now there are too many unanswered questions."

Fifteen minutes later Agent Baxter and some other agents reported to the Security Supervisor. "Sir … the original flight to Berlin has not been re-scheduled or cancelled. We have also ordered a no-fly order to the various airlines regarding the family."

"Good Agent Baxter. Now I guess we just have to wait for our eyes and ears to come in with some news. In the meantime I want to set up a task force to go over the classified data we have so far and next steps. We'll meet in ten minutes in the Olympus Room. I also want a team to contact any family, friends, neighbors, etc., that may have any information on the family's whereabouts. We'll be running this as a full Black Ops. We want the phone records, Twitter, Facebook … all the social media … everything."

"Yes Sir!" Agent Baxter responded.

Ten minutes later fifteen N.S.A. agents were in the Olympus Room reviewing the data so far. The meeting was barely three minutes in when a call came to the room.

A voice on the other end of the phone said, "Sir … we have located the vehicle at the San Jose Airport. We also now know the family purchased three extra tickets non-stop to Berlin Germany. Sir … you need to know that flight departed already and is in the air and en route. It is a non-stop flight Sir." He then told them the time the flight was scheduled to land in Berlin.

"Can you confirm they are on that flight?"

"One second Sir … yes Sir … it is confirmed those tickets were used and they are on the flight. We have all the information."

"Thank you and good work." The Security Supervisor then hung up.

Then the information was reported to the task force in the Olympus Room. "It has just been confirmed that the family is on a non-stop flight to Berlin Germany. We will inform our contacts in Berlin to make sure when that jet lands that the family is detained, questioned and returned to the United States. I'm going to fly to Berlin immediately on a Military jet and I will be taking a few of you with me. We should arrive before the Commercial jet lands. Now Agent Phoenix … what can you tell me about those mathematical formulas and data?" The Security Supervisor asked.

"Well Sir … I have had a chance to look over that data and the mathematics involved is at a level I am not familiar with. Also we just learned that someone or a group has breached our system and various other sites and was looking at a number of our defensive and offensive weapon systems … the classified material. Somehow they linked several systems together? Our computers were hacked in the area of communication capability systems, especially satellite capabilities and our ability to track and record Special OPS and the like. Mainly it was information gathering on our capabilities. We are still going over the data and we are going to have to call some top experts in the field to take a look at the mathematical formulas. Sir … I will tell you this is the real deal. This level of expertise is beyond what we have or I have ever experienced before? What is also disconcerting is the apparent ease the system was breached. Someone or some people are very, very proficient with computer systems and breaking encryptions and firewalls. At present I believe that our entire system could be at risk by this person or persons to breach it again. My understanding is that two of our agents were monitoring a suspect computer when we first became aware of this. We have had a short time to check further and Sir … I will tell you something. This is not the first time we have been breached by this computer. They have also breached some of our secure sites. As far as we know so far it has happened three times previously in the last eight months. That is about all I can tell you for now Sir."

"Good God!" The Security Supervisor was astonished. "We were aware some of our sites were being looked at when Baxter and White visited the family but not that our top secure sites were breached. This information will be passed up the chain of command to the Security Commander. And I am sure he will need to inform the President and the Secretary of Defense. The following will accompany me on a flight to Berlin. Baxter, Phoenix, White, Ramsay, Sanford, Diego and Chen. You can notify your families of your absence and that you will be gone for at least a couple of days. And usual protocols will be in force. No information disclosed beyond these doors unless approved. Any questions?"

There were no questions. Within forty-five minutes a high speed Military jet was boarded and was en route to Berlin Germany. The faces of all on board were focused on the success of this important mission. Which was of course the capture of their targets.

The Military jet sped along in the night sky across the ocean heading like a missile to Berlin. The speed of the jet at its near maximum as time was of the essence. They wanted to land before the commercial airliner touched down. They had contacted their Berlin contacts and the authorities were informed that there were three very important people on that commercial jet that were to be detained immediately upon landing. A Caucasian man about thirty years old, a Chinese woman about thirty years old, along with a four year old girl of mixed descent. There were no photographs, only descriptions for height, weight, age, etc. They could be travelling with counterfeit I.D. including passports? The ticket and seat numbers were passed along to the Berlin authorities. The arrests were to be made as covertly as possible.

The Military jet landed forty-five minutes before the commercial jet was to land. There was a brief meeting with local authorities and airport security. A sketch artist worked with Agent Baxter and Agent White because they had met the family during the house visit. Within twenty minutes copies of the wanted were made and passed on to the various security teams. They were all ready for the capture and waited for their Military jet to land in Berlin.

⌒⎜⎜⌒

On board the Commercial Airline all the passengers were asleep and getting some rest … all except one that is. Little Caitlin looked around at everyone asleep and was thinking. Thinking about who was coming and what must be done. She was tired but would sleep later. A few hours later and everyone began waking up and just in time too! The big jet had just started its descent when the captain came on the radio to announce their arrival and the local weather and thank the passengers for flying with them and the other usual spiel.

"Well … did you have a good sleep Caitlin?" Mommy asked the little girl.

"I slept a bit earlier Mommy. Almost everybody was sleeping on the jet. Even one of the pilots took a little snooze."

Both parents wondered how she knew that? "We are going to be on the ground soon Caitlin." Daddy said as he gave his little girl a hug and a kiss. "Looks like we are beginning to go down. We should be landing soon and then we can walk around and stretch our legs. Can anyone see the landing strip or airport?" He peered out the window.

Little Caitlin's eyes suddenly narrowed and her face changed to a scowl. She folded her little arms across the front of her chest. "They better watch out." Little Caitlin whispered under her breath but loud enough for both parents to hear her.

They immediately turned to look at their little girl. "Who better watch out?" Father asked.

Little Caitlin didn't answer. She just kept staring at one of the exit doors to the big jet. Her breathing increased.

"Who better watch out?" Mother asked this time. "Who are you talking about darling?"

Little Caitlin looked at Mommy and Daddy and growled softly, "Those people!" Her teeth were almost grinding as she bit down.

"What people Caitlin? What people are you talking about? Are there people at the airport waiting for us?" The Mother whispered back. Both parents showed sudden fear on their faces.

"Those people. They're baaaaad people. They just better watch out!" Caitlin blurted out as her little face became even more angry. "They have no idea what I can do! No idea at all!"

CHAPTER 7

THE HUNT: BERLIN

Exodus 34:12
"Watch yourself that you make no covenant with the inhabitants of the land into which you are going, or it will become a snare in your midst."

At the Berlin Airport they were ready. It wouldn't be long now. The message came in and was relayed to the team. Air France flight 1476 was on time and would be landing in fifteen minutes. Everyone was ready and so now it was just a matter of time before the N.S.A. agents had their suspects in custody. They waited, and waited, as time seemed to stand still. Their games faces were on.

The Security Supervisor for the N.S.A. sipped a coffee with Agent Baxter standing at his side. They both looked out the giant window into the sky for some sign … some sign the jet was coming to their trap. There was both relief and a nervous tension in the air surrounding them. They had them. There was no way they were going to get away. The parents had a lot to answer to. There would be many hard and difficult questions for the family. They were guilty in the eyes of the N.S.A. That's how they operate. That's how the cops operate too!

"It is because of moments like this that I love my job so much Baxter." The Security Supervisor stated. He never called an agent by their first name. It was always the last name. And the others always called him "Sir."

Agent Baxter just looked at him wondering what did he actually mean? "I love my job too Sir." She answered what really wasn't a question.

"I miss being in the field so when I get the opportunity I jump at the chance. And there is nothing better than the feeling of getting the bad guys. Protecting our Country … well … there is no higher honor … even when I was in the Marines and on the field of battle. This isn't quite the same but it is still quite the adrenalin rush. Don't you agree Baxter?" Her superior looking at her as his eyes peered over the top of the coffee cup. Agent Baxter suddenly thought his eyes looked … well … sinister under those circumstances.

"Yes Sir. There is that satisfaction of serving your Country … and the excitement." Agent Baxter was agreeing with her boss.

Just then several security personnel at the Schönefeld International Airport moved closer and informed the N.S.A. agents of the jet's status.

"Here they come Sir. See those lights in the sky? That would be the jet!" The airport supervisor said with a heavy German accent. "The passengers will be exiting the aircraft and coming down that long hallway." He pointed down the adjacent long hallway to his right. "We'll be ready. We have an area set aside for passengers to wait first before being permitted to leave. Just in case you need to question any of them?"

"Thank you Sir." The American eyed the German. The N.S.A. boss took one last quick sip of his coffee and put it down and he and the team all got into position and waited. Waited for the inevitable. The trap was set.

About fifteen minutes later the first passengers started to walk down the long hallway to the waiting agents and security personnel. Agent Baxter carefully studied the faces of each passenger and she was very thorough in her inspections. They all eyed each passenger as a possible enemy of the state. Minutes passed as more and more passengers exited the jet and entered the trap. The passengers were like a herd cattle being driven and funneled into a narrower and narrower enclosure to be inspected. It seemed to take forever. And then the number of passengers coming down the hallway started to thin out until the flow of passengers stopped. Then some members of the flight crew started to walk down the hallway towards them and were stopped by Security.

"Are there more passengers coming?" The N.S.A. Security Supervisor asked.

"No ... that's it. Everyone is off the jet Sir." She wondered what all the fuss was about?

Agent Baxter said, "I didn't see them Sir. Maybe they are hiding in the jet?"

The contingent of passengers were directed to the waiting area while Agent Baxter, her boss and a mix of several airport security and N.S.A. agents boarded the aircraft with some flight staff. A thorough search of the jet yielded no results. A panic started to come to the face of the Security Supervisor.

"Where are the passengers that were in seats 32D, 32E, and 32F? It was confirmed they were all on board at takeoff!" The Security Supervisor commanded.

A check on the passenger checklist and it was confirmed. Flight Attendants in that seating area were questioned as to the whereabouts of the three passengers seated in 32D, 32E, and 32F during the flight and at takeoff.

"No Sir. Those seats were empty and there were no passengers in those seats." The one Flight Attendant insisted. And it was the same answer from every personnel on the aircraft. When the sketches of the faces were shown to the aircraft staff none had seen those people ... or any little four-year old girl on the aircraft. A further check of the flight manifest showed they were supposed to be on board? The screening officers had checked them as boarded but they simply ... well ... seemed to have vanished?

"WHAT THE HELL IS GOING ON?" The N.S.A. boss yelled out in frustration and anger. "How the hell can your airline show them on board leaving an airport and when they land they are no longer on board?" He seemed to be yelling at everyone ... including his own staff. "Did they jump out of the bloody jet by fucken parachute?"

The Head of Security at the airport stated in a semi-calm voice, "Sir ... there can only be two possibilities. Either the passengers slipped by somehow ... which is impossible, or they were never on the jet but made it seem as if they were. Don't ask me how they did it because this has never happened before that I know of? And if Flight Personnel said they were never on the jet we know the answer don't we? They were never on the jet."

The N.S.A. Security Supervisor gave the Germans a dirty look and then walked off. It was like he was having a temper tantrum. Then he turned back to his team and yelled, "Baxter … get over here right now!" And then turned to walk away.

Agent Baxter walked off after her boss but first she said a "Thank you" to the German staff present and whispered a "Sorry" to them.

The Head of German Security told his team, "You can let all those passengers go. Tell them we are sorry for the delay. I imagine they are not very happy having to sit and wait for 45 minutes." Then he turned to one of his team members close by and said in a quieter voice, "Dass blutige amerikanische ist ein Arschloch." Then he added, "They made the mistake … not us! I am going to write a complaint about that guy! Piss on him!"

Baxter walked behind her boss and she knew he was pissed but it wasn't her fault. He better not start yelling at her though. She had never seen him so angry.

They went to a quiet area and he made the call back to the United States. "Sir …O'Reilly here. The targets were not on the jet. The Flight Crew confirmed they never were on the jet. I don't know how that happened and we need to find out but we do need to start looking again. They aren't here in Berlin!"

O'Reilly was listening to his boss … the Security Head Supervisor. "We know that now. We just became aware of that fact a few minutes ago. Some of our agents were looking at that computer video of the little girl and one of them noticed something. We investigated further and there is a partial image outside the window in the background. Upon further investigation we have confirmed it is the Eiffel Tower. And the background in the video is not in anyway the same as any part of the house. We are now quite certain that at the time of that observation by Baxter and the I.T. Agent that the Child … and family were actually in Paris France."

"What the hell?" O'Reilly thought for a second. "That would mean the image was sent via a remote connection to the computer in the house because that is the location we had for the transmission."

"We believe the same here. Pretty sophisticated stuff when you think about it and we have never been fooled … or rather misdirected like this before. We are examining the video closer and breaking it down. We may have another clue as to what we believe is a Hotel near the Eiffel Tower. You and your team are to board the Military jet and fly to Paris immediately. We are arranging the flight as we speak. We are also using our satellite imagery of the Paris area to see if we can spot them. Before you land in Paris we will be able to tell you the Hotel they are at … and hopefully the room number. There is a nine-hour difference in time zones so the suspects have a head start on us. Leave right now and brief your team O'Reilly." The Security Head Supervisor commanded.

"Yes Sir … right away." And then the phone line went dead.

Then O'Reilly turned to Baxter and said, "We are all going to Paris and we are all leaving immediately. I'll brief everyone once we are in the air."

O'Reilly called his N.S.A. team together and told them they would be leaving and flying to Paris immediately. The Military jet was ready and had already been refueled in the belief they would be heading back to United States with their captures.

As they walked through the airport O'Reilly saw the Head of German Security and went over and reluctantly said, "Ah… I need to apologize to you. You and your team didn't do anything wrong and on behalf of the United States of America I thank you for your services and assistance. Please accept my apologies."

The German gave a half smile and a half nod and replied, "That's okay." When the American was out of earshot the German gave a dirty look and simply said, "Arschloch!"

The N.S.A. team boarded the Military jet and then waited for permission to takeoff from the Berlin Airport Tower. It seemed to be taking longer than usual to get permission for takeoff. After a twenty-minute wait the pilot on the Military jet asked the Tower, "What is the holdup? We need to leave as soon as possible."

The traffic controller responded, "Yes Sir ... just another minute Sir and you will have clearance."

In the tower the Head of German Security was there. He thought about it for a minute. He had delayed the flight for a few minutes on purpose and finally shook his head in a yes nod and then the A.T.C.O. called the pilot back. "Military one four one cleared to Paris. You are now cleared for takeoff on runway Lucy 3."

"Berlin ground ... Military one four one ready to taxi IFR."

A minute later ... "Berlin tower ... Military one four one ready for takeoff IFR ... runway Lucy 3."

"Military one four one ... winds two eight zero at nine cleared for takeoff."

And then the Military jet was in the air and racing towards Paris. They would be in Paris within the hour.

Security Supervisor O'Reilly briefed his team. "Listen up! There have been some recent developments. Obviously we are all disappointed our targets were not on the Berlin jet but we have another chance. I will tell you that the initial Intel we received was incorrect. Our targets it seems were never on the jet. The airline somehow recorded the targets were on the jet. Regardless ... we now believe the targets are in Paris and that is our new destination. Our E.A. is fifty minutes. We will be receiving further information from Headquarters before we land as to the target's location. This Intel is recent and should be solid so make sure we are all ready to go. Any questions?"

Agent Baxter asked, "Do we know when and how they got to Paris? I am assuming the targets had counterfeit I.D. and passports. Otherwise we would have detected them in the system."

"At the moment we are looking at when and how the targets got to Paris. It seems your analysis of counterfeit I.D. and passports is likely what happened. We don't know how long the targets have been in Paris but what we do know is that we are only hours behind and we are close … very close to their last known location." O'Reilly then continued, "The French Authorities and the D.G.S.I. have been notified to be on the lookout for the targets in the Eiffel Tower area."

Then O'Reilly's phone rang. It was N.S.A. Headquarters in the United States. "O'Reilly … you are on the jet and en route to Paris. We are tracking you. Is it safe and secure to put me on intercom so I can speak to you and the team? We have some more information."

"Yes Sir. I will put you on speaker right now. You are on speaker to the team Sir."

"This is Security Head Supervisor Weatherly. The targets have been located at the Hotel de Londres Eiffel in Paris. The Hotel is about 550 yards from the Eiffel Tower. We have confirmed that the targets are still at the hotel and have not, I repeat … have not checked out yet. We believe our Intel to be solid. O'Reilly … I will give you the room number when I am finished speaking to the group. The French Authorities have been notified of our arrival and they have the hotel secured and under surveillance. This is an important mission and I want everyone to be ready to go. We are sending you a map of the Hotel so you can plan for a successful mission. Good luck and O'Reilly … let me know when you have them."

"Yes Sir and we await the map of the Hotel." O'Reilly answered.

"Wait a minute." Weatherly stated and after a 30 second pause Weatherly added. "Okay ... I was just checking if any new Intel came in but nothing new. I will keep you informed. The targets should be fairly easy to zero though with the Child and the Chinese mother. You are instructed to return all three to the United States as soon as possible. Interrogation will take place here. That is all. We are sending the map now." And then the phone call ended.

CHAPTER 8

THE SPIDER'S WEB: PARIS

Psalm 31:15

"My times are in your hand; rescue me from the hand of my enemies and from my persecutors!"

Little Caitlin continued to stare at the exit door as the jet approached the runway in Paris.

"Caitlin ... are you saying there are people waiting for us when the jet lands?" Mommy whispered so no other passengers could hear.

"No ... they aren't here yet but they are planning to come for us. We're okay Mommy and Daddy but they are going to try and capture us. I don't like that. I won't let that happen. They better watch out!" Caitlin said in a very soft voice. Her face though showed her anger.

"Okay ... that's good Caitlin. The people chasing us are somewhere else. How do you know that though?" The father asked.

"I don't know how to explain it Daddy. It is like breathing to me. I just think about it and then I ... kind of see it ... or feel it. I see things that impact me mostly but I can see things that impact others if I concentrate. I am still learning how to do it and I am getting better and better every day at it."

"We have a lot of questions to ask you Caitlin but first what did you mean when you said they better watch out and they have no idea what you can do?" The mother asked the question with a sick feeling in her stomach. The Daddy and Mommy both felt uneasy in what their little girl had said. They had tried their best to teach their daughter to be good ... to be fair ... to be understanding of other people's differences in every way ... and to show kindness.

"I know you have a lot of questions Mommy and Daddy." She was looking directly at her parents. "I have laid some spider webs down though and they will have some trouble finding us. You ask me what can I do? I haven't told you everything Mommy and Daddy. Sorry but I don't want to overwhelm you." The little girl could speak as well or rather better than any adult if need be. Around others she was wise to still pretend she was a normal little four-year old girl and acted accordingly. She talked more like an adult to her parents most times … though at times the little girl in her still showed. "I won't tell you now … this is not the right time but I can do some things … that … well … would frighten a lot of regular people. You and Daddy aren't regular people though. I will be good but you need to know that I will protect both of you … and myself should I need to. I want to talk with both of you more at the Hotel … in private. I will tell you more. I love you Mommy and Daddy."

Both parents sat back in silence thinking about what their little girl had just said. It was a lot to swallow. As the father sat there thinking about all that he heard … his mind was racing. Then he thought of something and asked his little girl sitting beside him. "Caitlin … can you read people's minds? Can you read our minds?"

Caitlin looked at Daddy … then at Mommy and then at Daddy again and answered, "Not read minds in the way you think but I can definitely sense things. It's not words so much that I hear or see but a sense of …uhm … like an instinct. I just feel it I guess? Like someone touching your arms … except for me it is like someone touching my brain."

"Aaahhh." The father wasn't quite sure what to think of that answer?

Little Caitlin just laughed at the look on her Daddy's face. She had such a cute innocent face. No one would know by looking at her just how special this little girl was … or how dangerous. Even her parents didn't fully understand. They were learning more everyday though.

"This is my first plane ride or rather jet ride." Little Caitlin suddenly blurted out. "It is kind of cool but it sure is slow."

Mommy gave a little laugh. It broke the serious mood. "Caitlin … we just crossed the ocean in a few hours. We are travelling about 500 miles per hour. You call that slow?"

"Yes ... very, very slow ... like a snail travels. Phone calls are much faster. That is how humans should travel on Earth Mommy."

"People can't travel like that Caitlin. At least not yet and what did you mean on Earth?"

"No Daddy ... people can't travel like that yet ... but they could. And I think they could do so much more. It would be so simple. Space travel would be different though ... compared to Earth travel."

Both parents looked at their daughter in shock. Caitlin gave a little smirk. "There is so much I could do here on Earth." She gave a deep sigh. Both parents wondered what she meant by "Here on Earth?" Just then the tires of the big jet touched the runway. They were in Paris. After passing security at the Charles de Gaulle Airport the father asked about taxi service and after twenty minutes there was a taxi in front of them.

"Où veux-tu aller?" The taxi driver asked.

"What did you say Sir?" The father looked at the taxi driver.

"He asked where do you want to go Daddy?" Little Caitlin quickly acted as the interpreter.

"Oh ... I'm sorry Monsieur. I can speak English. The little girl is right ... where would you like to go?"

"Nous emmener à l'hôtel de londres." Little Caitlin quickly blurted out as she gave a little giggle.

"Your French is very, very good." The taxi driver answered in surprise. "Your little girl speaks very good French. Even the accent is very good."

"Yes she does." Then the mother leaned over and whispered in her daughter's ear. "Try not to draw attention to yourself."

Little Caitlin had a questioning look on her face but cupped her one tiny hand and put it to her Mommy's ear and simply whispered back, "Okay Mommy."

Lots of traffic in Paris but the taxi was definitely the way to travel. It took about fifty minutes for them to arrive at the hotel. The family paid the taxi driver and thanked him very much. They certainly were travelling light … very little luggage. They registered fairly quickly and got the keys to their room. Soon they were in their room and even though they wanted to explore Paris a bit and eat they needed a little rest first. They were quite tired … especially little Caitlin and so they decided to take a short nap and set the alarm for two hours. They put the do not disturb sign on the door. They all fell asleep quite quickly. In no time at all the alarm went off and they all woke up. They decided to order room service and ordered a pepperoni pizza. No mushrooms. Little Caitlin and Mommy didn't like mushrooms. Daddy liked mushrooms but he was out voted. He didn't mind though. They had fruit for dessert.

After eating the family decided to go out and Caitlin wanted to see the Eiffel Tower since it is a famous landmark and was so close by. Caitlin was already an expert after reading about it once a few years ago. It only took her about ten seconds to read and learn everything there was to know about the Eiffel Tower. The family walked to the Eiffel Tower. It was only a short distance away from the Hotel. Once there they went to the top, or rather near the top. It took a long time because of the line-ups but once at the top the view was spectacular.

"We are about a thousand feet in the air Mommy and Daddy. We can see for a long way and we can see much of the city. There is our hotel over there." Caitlin pointed down to the ground. Caitlin held on to Sally … her little rag doll. It was a long way down to the ground below.

"We are certainly high off the ground." The father stated. He was not so much a fan of being high off the ground like this. For some reason a plane or jet felt safer than this old structure.

"You're safe Daddy … its been standing a long, long time. Did you know it takes over fifty metric tons of paint and they repaint it every seven years. Imagine having to physically paint this thing? The painters have no fear of heights. Caitlin then proceeded to tell Mommy and Daddy all about the Eiffel Tower." Little Caitlin was acting as a tour guide again.

"Let's just enjoy the view for a few more minutes and then go back to the hotel." The father tried his best to redirect his daughter.

"The views pretty cool but the air stinks here. I can tell their air pollution indexes are in the mid-80's right now." Caitlin happened to blurt out.

An old man standing nearby asked the little girl, "How do you know the pollution index?" An old couple had been listening to the little girl talk about the Eiffel Tower and were amazed that she knew so much.

"Oh … we were reading all about it before we brought her up here." The mother answered. "Well … we better go now."

"Oh." The old man said as the family was rushing off. "You certainly have a smart little girl there!" He seemed to shout out to them as they hurried away.

Back in the room they decided to talk … and plan. And the parents wanted more information on what their daughter meant when she said on the jet, "They have no idea what I can do?"

Mommy asked the question. "What did you mean when you said they have no idea what you can do? Remember you promised no freezing or boiling of their blood?"

"Yes ... I remember the promise Mommy. I am not exactly sure of all the things I can do? I am learning and finding out ... sometimes by accident. I think I've figure out something that can really help us but I am still new at controlling it."

The Mommy asked under bated breath, "What can you control?"

"Well ... I was thinking about time. It has to do with Einstein's Theory of Relativity and time travel but not really. And you know I read Tesla's work and others. That's old school though. Anyway ... I started wondering if time travel was really a possibility? So I thought more and more about it and was figuring things out. Anyway, what I found out was I can control time and I think time may be one of the most powerful things in the universe if that is true. So what I did was stop time but only for a few seconds. No one noticed ... except me that is." Caitlin tried to explain to her parents.

"What do you mean you stopped time Caitlin? I don't understand?" The Daddy asked.

"I did it the other day ... just as an experiment but only for a few seconds though ... time stopped." Caitlin answered looking at Mommy and Daddy's astonished faces.

"No one can stop time Caitlin. You must be mistaken." The mother tried to tell her daughter. "Maybe you are mistaken?"

"No Mommy ... I am not mistaken ... and I did stop time but only in our old neighborhood the other day. I didn't stop the Earth rotating or the path around the Sun. I'm not sure if I can do that yet? I need to work out the possible repercussions before I think about trying that. And really I don't think I need to do that. That will take some more time to figure out." The little girl spoke as if it was just an every day simple occurrence. The parents didn't really believe Caitlin was serious about stopping the Earth's rotation. They thought ...

or rather they were hoping that it was just in the little girl's imagination? Then again this time thing was something entirely unexpected.

"Just how do you know time stopped Caitlin?" Daddy asked not believing his daughter. This couldn't possible be true.

"Well … I did stop time and everything kind of froze for a few seconds but without the temperature drop." Caitlin made sure to reassure her Mommy she didn't freeze everything temperature wise. She was watching her parents and saw this might be too much for them to take in right now … perhaps later.

"So … you think you … made time stop … in the old neighborhood?" Daddy struggled to understand and believe.

"Yes. I well … stopped the time and everything stopped. For example … the people … birds … bugs … trees and plants and only in that particular grid zone that I set up. And I only did it for 2.5 seconds on the clocks. I rounded it off to the nearest tenth of a second. So what I kind of meant was that if those bad people come I will freeze time so we can get away but I am not exactly sure how long I can freeze it yet? I am afraid to try until I work out any possible negative complications. I really would rather not hurt anyone." Caitlin did not tell her parents some of the other new abilities she had. She could do way more than just simply freeze time.

"Holy shit!" The father blurted out. "This is some serious sci-fi movie stuff here if this is true."

"Hey Daddy! No swearing … remember?" Caitlin shook her index finger at her Daddy.

"You aren't kidding Michael. This is extremely shocking." The mother added.

"I know Mommy but the more you become aware of things maybe those things will be less shocking to you? Do you want me to show you that I can freeze time? I won't freeze you and Daddy this time. Then you could see it." Caitlin suggested to her parents.

"NO! Let's leave time alone. At least for now Caitlin … okay?" Mother was quick to respond.

"Okay … I won't show you now. You shouldn't be afraid though. I'm going to go on the computer for a bit. I have some things I need to research."

She gave Mommy a big hug and kiss and then the same for her Daddy and they were longer than the usual hugs. Then Caitlin went on the computer they bought a couple of hours before the flight across the ocean. Caitlin logged in and connected to the web and was soon on the N.S.A. site. Except this wasn't the public site but the secure site. There wasn't any firewall or security capable of stopping little Caitlin. She found it so easy to break in. In the last few months she had visited the secure sites of the C.I.A., the F.B.I., and well … lots of so-called secure sites … even in other Countries. And they weren't even aware they were breached … at least not yet. Caitlin was on the N.S.A. site looking at the top-secret satellite capabilities and designs … and in a different box she was working on some simple mathematical equations when she suddenly became aware of something. She should have noticed it earlier but she noticed the web camera was on … without the red notification light on. She quickly reversed and tracked the signal in a Nano-second and saw just who it was. It was that lady Baxter from the N.S.A. and some other man. Caitlin quickly disconnected … pushed several keys to send to the computer back at the old house that she was connected to as a clone sight and then shutdown the computer.

Then she yelled out, "Mommy! … Daddy! … We are leaving right now! Let's go!"

CHAPTER 9

N.S.A. ARRIVES: CLOSING IN

Luke 6:31
"And as you wish that others would do to you, do so to them."

The Military jet with the N.S.A. team was making its approach into Paris. They had planned every contingency down to the last minutest detail. There was no room for error. The French Authorities had set up perimeter checks around the Hotel and were ordered to be as discreet as possible. That was impossible though as there were so many uniformed police there it looked like a battleground. The N.S.A. didn't want the family to be aware what was happening. They wanted the element of surprise. This time there would be no escape for the family.

The Military jet touched down and soon the N.S.A. agents were riding in assigned vehicles and making their way to the Hotel. They arrived by police escort in about thirty minutes. As the vehicles approached they turned off their flashing lights when they were close to the Hotel. The escort vehicles stopped in front of the Hotel and the N.S.A. team excited the vehicles.

O'Reilly called his team together. They were dressed better and more prepared than any S.W.A.T. team one could imagine. "I am looking for Inspector Guerrier." O'Reilly called to a group of French authorities.

A man answered to his left, "I am Inspecteur Guerrier. You are O'Reilly?" The Inspecteur was standing almost right beside him.

"Yes Inspector … I am O'Reilly. I was told you are my contact and that you were informed earlier by the N.S.A that we believe there are three suspects staying at the hotel. There is a married couple … a white male about thirty years old … a female of Chinese descent about thirty years old and they are travelling with their four-year-old daughter. Our latest Intel is that they are still at the Hotel. We believe they are travelling using counterfeit passports and identifications under the names Jim Gray, Lila Gray and daughter Amanda Gray." He spoke to a group of about ten French Authorities with the Inspector.

"Do you believe the suspects are armed and dangerous?" The Inspecteur asked.

"We don't know what to expect so regular protocols should be in place as they could be armed and dangerous? I do want all your officers to be aware and to be very careful, as there is a young Child present. We especially do not want the Child harmed in any way. That is imperative." O'Reilly emphasized making it quite clear.

"Yes ... I understand. I will inform the team. Perin!" The Inspecteur called out to an officer in the group, "Relay that message to all members of the team."

"Oui Inspecteur Guerrier." Perin confirmed and then reminded the French team that there was a Child in the group and that shooting should be a last resort. They were professionals and knew what to expect and to always be on the ready.

"I'd like you and some of your team to come with us to the front desk to confirm what room the suspects are in." The Inspecteur asked O'Reilly.

O'Reilly nodded and then called to his team, "Baxter, Ramsay, Diego, Chen ... you'll come with us to the front desk and then to the room. Phoenix, White ... you two stay and watch the front entrance. Sanford I want you at the elevator doors and watch the lobby area ... just in case. I don't need to remind you to keep your ears and eyes open."

Then O'Reilly turned to speak to Guerrier and said, "We believe they have a room on the 6th floor in the Room Jean de LA FONTAINE but we will go to the front desk to inquire about the three suspects and to verify if they are in the room or out and about somewhere else."

Inspecteur Guerrier nodded in agreement. The Americans and the French immediately set up for the capture and they walked into the Hotel and approached the front service desk. All the desk clerks saw the group of officers approaching and wondered what was going on?

"Je suis inspecteur Guerrin. Nous pensons qu'il peut y avoir une famille de trois rester ici sous le nom de Gris ou Brennan. Sont-ils séjournaient ici et dans quelle pièce sont-ils? Savez-vous sont l'invité actuellement dans leur chambre?"

"I just told the clerk who I was and that we believe a family of three is staying here and may be registered under the names Gray or Brennan and we want him to check what room they are registered in? I also asked if they knew if the guests were presently in the room." The Inspecteur informed the American.

O'Reilly answered, "Yea … I know. Thanks. I speak a bit of French."

"Okay … that is good." The Inspecteur nodded.

The head desk clerk answered in English. "Yes … we have a family of three registered in Room Jean de La Fountaine under the name Gray. They are not scheduled to check out until tomorrow. I will ring the phone if you want to see if they are in the room?"

"No! Don't do that until we are upstairs and at the room door. We don't want them to get suspicious, as they know we are looking for them and they might panic and run. We will need a room key in case they won't open the door. We will let you know when to ring the phone and we will listen at the door. We don't expect any trouble but we should be ready for it just the same." O'Reilly was adamant. He was trying not to upset the guests. He feared the team needed to move fast before too many people in the Hotel were aware there was some problem with so many police at the Hotel.

"Very well … I will wait for the signal before ringing the room." The head desk clerk answered as he looked around. He was starting to get even more worried.

Some of the team members then went up the stairs. Some went in the elevator to the 6th floor. Once on the 6th floor they moved quickly to the room and stood listening at the door for any signs someone was inside. They heard a television on inside the room. There was a "ne pas déranger" or a "Do Not Disturb" sign hanging on the door handle. When they were ready they called downstairs for the clerk to ring the room. When the suspects answered the phone he was to say he was the Hotel manager and that as a courtesy he was just checking to see if the family was enjoying their stay at the Hotel de Londres Eiffel. When the suspects answered the phone that would be the signal when the team would rush the room. If the door was locked from inside they would pound on the door identifying themselves and if no one opened the door, the officers would use the key or if necessary break the door down and apprehend the suspects.

Then the phone could be heard ringing in the room. The agents listened outside waiting for someone to answer, their heart rates increasing as they listened to the ringing of the phone inside. The phone rang and rang but no one answered. After the sixth ring the Inspecteur pounded on the door identifying who they were and within seconds opened the door with the room key. They rushed the room in what seemed exactly like some movie scene. Guns drawn … lots of shouting but the suspects were not there. Further inspection revealed there were no clothes, suitcases or personal belongings of any kind in the room although the television was on. Did the suspects just leave a short time ago not even turning off the television? Perhaps they were out at supper or sightseeing but there were no personal belongings in the room? The two keys to the room were left on the table in the room near the front door. It seemed the suspects had left and perhaps left rather quickly? When did they leave and if so how much of a head start did they have?

"What the Hell? What kind of bullshit is this?" O'Reilly was beginning to show his anger again. This was the second time that the N.S.A. had thought they had cornered the suspects and each time they seemed to have escaped mysteriously?

Guerrin said to O'Reilly, "Sir … we need to ask at the front desk and talk with the various staff at the Hotel to see if we can find anything out about the family. The suspects obviously somehow knew you and your team were coming and seem to have left the Hotel. Perhaps they are nearby? I suggest we contact the taxi services, busses, and hotel staff to ascertain if they have any information about the family? The Hotel has cameras and we should view the recorded video to see when they left … what they were wearing and try to determine where they were going? I will direct my team to start immediately."

Agent Baxter added, "And … I should review the Hotel videos immediately as we may get a clear picture of them and the first thing we need to do is to make sure that the family that stayed in this room are indeed the targets. We are pretty sure they are though and as the Inspecteur stated we need to determine when they left … how they left and their destination?"

O'Reilly agreed and immediately informed Agent Sandford, Phoenix and White who were still stationed downstairs that the suspects were not in the room and may or may not be in the Hotel but to keep their eyes and ears open.

O'Reilly reiterated, "Agent Baxter and I will talk with the Manager as we have been informed the suspects have not checked out but with no luggage or personal belongings in the room it is obvious they left some time ago? There must be someone who saw them leave the Hotel and at what time they left?"

Inspecteur Guerrier replied, "Yes … I will accompany you to talk with the Hotel Manager on duty and we can ask about the videos. I noticed they have cameras in the hallway and elevator and at the front entrance. We should be able to get a good clear picture of the suspects."

So they went down to the front desk. Inspecteur Guerrier asked the clerk at the registration desk if he could speak to the Hotel Manager immediately. The clerk called the Manager to the front desk stating the police wanted a word with him. A Monsieur Lafleur introduced himself as the Manager on duty.

"Yes Sir. How can I be of service to you?"

The Inspecteur asked Monsieur Lafleur about the family that was supposed to be staying in the Room Jean de LA FONTAINE on the 6th floor. "There are guests staying in that room and when we went to the room we noticed the room was unoccupied although the television was left on. We need any information you may have regarding those guests and we need it quickly."

"Very well Inspecteur. I will check again but I don't believe they have checked out." Lafleur confirmed with his staff at the front desk and they confirmed that the family had not checked out yet.

"Was there a young girl with them about four years old and the mother was Chinese?" O'Reilly asked the Manager.

"Yes … they were very polite but very quiet. The little girl always seemed to have a rag doll with her. If I remember it was the little girl that asked me some questions. I was here when they arrived a few days ago. I believe it was Wednesday? Yes … it was Wednesday and they reserved the room for three days. They still have the room until tomorrow morning."

"You have video of their arrival and their departure? We need to look at that right now!" Inspecteur Guerrier stated.

"Well … I remember their arrival but just before they arrived our power went out in the hotel so all our video shutdown. It was only off for about twenty minutes? Funny thing was that our Hotel was the only building in the area that the power went off … which is quite strange? Our emergency lights came on but there is no video at the time they arrived. That was Wednesday just after 4:00 P.M. I called an electrician even though the power came back on but he found nothing wrong with the electrical system?" Lafleur told the Inspecteur.

"The power went off just before they arrived?" Agent Baxter looked at her boss in disappointment. "We will need to look at those videos. Did they go out that you know of during their stay? They seemed to have left the Hotel?"

"Yes … they mentioned going to the Eiffel Tower and I believe they went there a short time after their arrival? They were gone for about two or three hours? I remember because I was on duty and saw them leave. Now that I think of it the power went off again at about the same time they left? I remember clearly because I have worked here at the Hotel for twenty-one years and we have never had such strange power outages? The electrician and hydro company could not explain why it kept happening?"

Lafleur took O'Reilly, Baxter, the Inspecteur and another French Policeman to a back room to view videos in the hope of seeing the suspects. After an hour of fast-forwarding the videos without success O'Reilly received a call from the N.S.A. Headquarters from his boss, Security Head Supervisor Weatherly.

Weatherly asked, "Do you have the suspects in custody?"

"No Sir we do not. It appears the suspects somehow got wind we were coming to the Hotel. When we got here we met with the French Authorities … then went directly to the Hotel and stormed the room but the room was vacated. No luggage or personal belongings. They haven't checked out yet. Presently we are asking Hotel staff and gathering information about the suspects and when they left or where they might be? Agent Baxter and I and Inspector Guerrier and a member of his team are looking at the Hotel videos to see if we can get a clear image of the suspects."

"Well … that is disappointing. We now know the suspects left on an earlier flight under an alias from the San Jose Airport to Paris on Tuesday. We are checking videos at the airport but so far no luck. The videos were either down or tampered with somehow during their departure." Weatherly told O'Reilly.

"We seem to have the same problem here Sir. They must have some kind of jamming device to shut video or power down."

"I should tell you O'Reilly that we ordered a financial freeze of their assets ... their bank accounts but all those accounts are no longer there. Their monies have been transferred from their accounts. We are tracking now where the money went. They'll be a trail and we will find it. We also cancelled their credit cards but I believe they have other credit cards they are using." Weatherly was frustrated as well. "Let me know when you have any more information." Weatherly said in a commanding voice.

"Yes Sir I will."

Then Lafleur remembered something. "I should tell you that our power also went off this morning ... at about 7:30 A.M. I was not on duty at the time but since we have been having electrical problems and we don't know why it is a big concern for us here at the Hotel."

Just then both O'Reilly and Guerrier's received information at almost the same time. Both were told the exact same information by a member of their respective teams.

Agent Sandford told O'Reilly, "Sir ... the Hotel doorman who was on duty this morning but is now at home was contacted by phone and he remembers quite clearly that the family left at 7:33 A.M. this morning. He believes they were going to the TGV Lyria Train Station. Sir ... the little girl was with them and he remembers her because well ... she spoke English, French and Chinese. She was speaking Chinese to her parents. He said she seemed quite the smart little girl and he mentioned she had a rag doll with her."

"Bloody shit." O'Reilly blurted out to everyone within earshot. "That means they are still several hours in front of us. Do you know where those trains go? O'Reilly asked the Inspector.

"The TGV Lyria goes to Geneva, Zurich, Lausanne, Basil, and Bern. They are all in Switzerland. Those train rides are all about three to four hours travel time. There are airports in all those cities except Basil. If they are there you can save some time by flying. First we need to check with the train station to confirm their destination? You should get your team together fast and get in the vehicles and we will escort you there. I will call the train station en route to let them know we are coming and also ask about the family and if anyone remembers them."

The Inspecteur received another call and then told the American, "We may have some luck on our side. The doorman remembered the taxi company and upon checking it has been reported the fare was taken to the train station back at the airport. I am going to send a couple of my men to the taxi company to speak with the driver."

"Fuck, fuck, fuck." O'Reilly said rather loudly. "I hope they didn't get on another jet somewhere. If they took the train at least that would slow them down a bit and we might be able to gain some time catching up with them." Then O'Reilly added, "That sounds like a good plan of action Inspector so let's get in the vehicles and get to the train station as fast as we can." O'Reilly gave a very big sigh after speaking. O'Reilly called his team to meet at the front door of the Hotel immediately. Guerrier did the same for his team. The N.S.A. team followed the French Police as they raced back to the airport where the train station was.

CHAPTER 10

SWITZERLAND: THE STRANGER

Matthew 25:35
"For I was hungry and you gave me food, I was thirsty and you gave me drink, I was a stranger and you welcomed me,"

The family abruptly left the Hotel, and then headed to the train station. It was a planned escape although slightly ahead of the expected time. Now the planning of the escape was not so much by the parents but by little Caitlin. She was tired though. She was after all only four years old … although her incredible intelligence deluded all that heard her speak. She was also starting to get angrier and angrier towards her pursuers. She developed her instincts for survival based on what Mommy and Daddy taught her. That all life … no matter what it was … was a special gift never to be abused or belittled. But the little girl was beginning to learn something else. She knew it before but now … it was becoming even more apparent to her. And that was that there was evil in the World. Real evil and that there were bad people … people who justified what they would do … or could do without an afterthought of consequences. They justified their actions no matter what. The little girl was realizing that for whatever crazy reason she and she alone had the incredible power to change all that. Her dilemma was how to change it without becoming the evil herself. She realized at even that young tender age that would be her greatest temptation. That people were not like insects or some unimportant life form. Still her anger worried her to some extent. No one had any idea of the sheer power she possessed even now … and it was growing stronger and stronger every day. Even little Caitlin was not aware of her true powers and those yet to come.

Caitlin knew the taxi had a video camera. They were easy to take out as nonfunctional. Just as she shutdown the various cameras on the streets and the satellites above her that were trying to take pictures of her or track her. She sensed what the N.S.A. was attempting to do at the instant they were trying to do it. Her parents were oblivious to many of these facts or at least they were oblivious for now as to what their little girl was actually doing behind the scenes. The parents were showing the stress too! Caitlin sensed it.

She spoke to her parents in the Chinese language. Her Daddy was partially fluent and he spoke fairly good Chinese. Her Mommy was fluent though. Mandarin was her first language after all when she was growing up in China. The little girl spoke the Standard Chinese language, the Putonghua, which was a form of the Mandarin dialect to her parents. That is what they understood although the little girl was fluent in all the so-called "Living Languages" in China … all 292 of them. She had a thirst for knowledge and there were actually very few languages on the planet she was not totally fluent in and she wanted to learn every single language … especially the dying languages of some of the minority groups on Earth. She also wanted to know the cursor or writing parts of the languages as well.

Little Caitlin briefed her parents on the way to the train station what to expect and had earlier told them in private where they were going. She didn't want the taxi driver to hear what she was saying as she already knew the police and the N.S.A. people would be talking with him later. So she spoke the Mandarin language.

"Everything is okay Mommy and Daddy. Soon we will be on the train and then we will disappear for a while. That will be when we can rest and not be worried so much about them … the bad people finding us."

The parents nodded in reply as the little girl spoke. In a short time they were at the train station and got out of the taxi and got their meager luggage. They thanked the taxi driver. Then they bought three one-way tickets to Zurich, Switzerland. The timing was perfect as the train was just about to depart.

"It won't be long now Mommy and Daddy. We'll be in Zurich in four hours and three minutes on this high-speed train. Enjoy the ride."

The father was worried though and so he whispered to his little miracle Child, "Those people … are they chasing us Caitlin?" The mother was listening and waiting for the answer also.

"Yes … they are trying to follow us but I have not made it easy and try not to worry. They are hours behind us. We will be in Zurich before they realize we are not at the Paris Hotel." Little Caitlin whispered back so no one would hear.

They were about one hour into the train ride when the little girl started to look at a man three seats in front of her and on the opposite side. The stranger had his back to her and was travelling alone. Caitlin kept staring at him and … well … seemed to be thinking about something.

The mother noticed her daughter's interest in the man and leaned down and whispered, "What is it Caitlin? You keep looking at that man up there in the grey suit. Is something wrong? Is everything all right?"

Caitlin looked at her Mommy … then at her Daddy who was actually catching a snooze. He looked funny slouched over in the seat. The seats were nice though. They were fairly comfortable.

"Everything is fine Mommy but that man … he is interesting. I think I want to talk with him."

"Why do you want to talk with him Caitlin? He is a stranger you know and we must be careful … you must be careful. What is so interesting about him?"

"There are some very interesting things about this man Mommy." Little Caitlin turned her eyes towards her Mommy for only a second before turning back to look at the man.

Just then the father woke up as he heard part of the conversation. "What's going on?" He looked at his daughter, his wife, and then the passengers around him.

"Caitlin wants to talk with that man over there." The Mommy pointed with her eyes. "The man is sitting three seats up on the other side wearing the grey suit."

"Why do you want to talk with that man honey?"

"I can think of two main reasons ... well ... actually three main reasons. Yes ... I will need to talk with that man. I am sure of it now." The little girl looked directly at Daddy ... then back at Mommy.

"What do you mean? What are the reasons?" Mommy asked.

"I will tell you two of the reasons. The third reason I will wait before I decide what needs to be done. The first reason is he is a scientist and a member of the S.S.C.N. I find the Swiss Stem Cells Network interesting and for that reason I want to talk with him." Little Caitlin whispered.

Daddy asked, "How do you know he is a member of the Swiss Stem Cells Network honey? Did you see his picture somewhere?"

"Yes ... I remember his picture and biography but that isn't all of it. I sensed it when I scanned the passengers on the train. I detected his thoughts as he was thinking about some particular stem cell research right now. He isn't quite right with the research and he is a bit off track. But there is even a more important reason I want to talk with him Daddy."

"Oh my GOD Caitlin. You can do that? Scan and read people's brain and thoughts?" The Mommy blurted out. "I know you said you could do it a little bit before but now you say you scanned the people on the train?"

"Mommy ... Daddy ... I said I was getting better and better at it and that is true. I try not to read other people's thoughts and I am better at controlling the ... noise of all those thoughts. Much of it is ... well ... just random useless thoughts ... what should I make for supper? I hope my wife doesn't find out I cheated on her? Stuff I am not interested in very much. However ... the intellectual stuff that has importance ... well ... that interests me ... and that man over there interests me."

"Wow!" The Daddy blurted out. "Caitlin … what is the second reason for wanting to talk with that man?"

The little girl looked at her Mommy and Daddy and then stated, "Because he is connected to the Holocaust."

Mommy and Daddy stared in shock at what their little girl just said.

"Jesus Bloody Christ!" The Daddy couldn't control what he suddenly let slip.

"Daddy! Your language!" Little Caitlin frowned at her Daddy.

"Sorry honey. You come out of the blue with some pretty crazy pieces of information." The Daddy apologized. "How could you possibly know he is connected to the Holocaust? I mean in what way is he connected?"

"His father and grandparents and some family members. That is how he is connected. Some of his family was at Auschwitz and perished there. I want to talk to him not so much about that but because he is a scientist and he is a supporter of the persecuted. He will be a sympathizer and ally to us. That is my sense of him." Caitlin stated matter of fact. "Now Mommy … I want you to take me over there to speak with him. Daddy you come too but after we get settled. And it would be better if you both just … well … let me talk. He is going to be in shock after hearing what I have to say." Little Caitlin was smiling and what a cute smile she had. No one would guess by looking at her what was on her inner side. That is for sure.

And at that the little girl and Mommy got up to go and sit near the stranger man. He looked at them for a second, gave a little smile but then went back to reading his papers and writing on his notepad, as he was deep in thought. The Daddy came over just a few seconds later.

"Excuse me Sir. We are sorry for bothering you but you see … my daughter here," the Mommy looked at her daughter with love, "well … she was insistent on meeting you. I will tell you Sir that you are probably going to remember this morning for the rest of your life."

"Well … what a strange thing to say … but I do need to give my eyes a break so I guess I can spare a few minutes?" The stranger said as he squinted his eyes through his semi-thick framed glasses while looking at the family. "What's your daughter's name?"

The little girl answered, "My name is … let's just say it is Kirsten." Mommy and Daddy stared at their daughter in surprise at the name change?

"Well … hello Kirsten … and how old are you?" The strange man asked.

"I am four and a half years old Dr. Froehlich."

"My … I can tell you are smart and only being four and a half years old but how do you know my name? Do I know you somehow?" The stranger leaned forward.

"No … we have never met before but we are connected in more ways than you know. Now what I am about to reveal to you … well … you must make me a promise."

"A promise? Hmmm?" The stranger said somewhat amused but definitely he was curious. "What's the promise?" He was smiling as he thought all this was … well … strange?

"That you will remain calm and covert about what I am about to tell you."

"Okay … I promise to remain calm and covert." The stranger answered with his eyebrows showing his curiosity as he looked at the Child and then at the parents. He had certainly never heard a Child use the word covert before?

"Ah … are you absolutely sure about this Kirsten." Daddy asked his little girl. He almost used the name Caitlin but he didn't.

"Yes … I am quite sure about this Daddy."

"Now … what is this about?" The stranger asked as he leaned forward even more.

"You are Dr. Lucas Froehlich and you work at the Swiss Stem Cells Network. I know how strange this is going to sound but you have been studying for some time now not just stem cell research but the idea of intelligence of the brain and cell replacement therapies and disease modeling … " But then Caitlin or rather Kirsten was interrupted.

"Whoa … is this some kind of joke? You are only four years old and you are starting to talk to me like a colleague would? Who put you up to this?" The doctor was having trouble believing a little girl could talk like that.

"Dr. Froehlich … this is no joke … our little girl is not like anyone you will ever meet in your entire life. I really suggest you listen to her. I have a feeling everything you thought you knew is about to change forever." The Daddy interjected.

The doctor just looked very perplexed and began looking even more closely at the little girl.

"Thanks Daddy but I will take it from here. I love you Daddy." Caitlin snuck that in. "Okay … so I have to tell you something before we go any further. I know all about your work and the work of your many colleagues. What I am going to tell you will be shocking to you. I know you have the conference coming up soon in Geneva but more than that I know you are kind of on the right track for your research but … and excuse me for saying this … you are not quite on the right course of action. You've been studying the development of the neural crest, a transient population of cells in higher vertebrates that emigrates from the developing neural tube to generate most of the peripheral nervous system and a variety of non-neural structures. Those neural crest stem cells or NCSCs that display self-renewal capacity and multi-potency in clonal cell culture assays. You've also been able to isolate cells very similar to NCSCs from neural crest-derived structures during fetal development and even from adult tissues such as the skin. I am referring to those transcription factors and signaling pathways that regulate self-renewal and fate decisions in NCSCs. Now you are trying to include potential therapeutic applications of adult neural crest-derived stem cells and the study of disease mechanisms involving aberrant neural crest stem cell development and tumor formations. In the human melanoma cells and those genetic mouse models of melanoma, there has only been some substantiation of the role of stem cell features for tumor initiation, growth, and metastasis formation, so by studying processes of normal stem cell development it looks like a promising path towards the elucidation of mechanisms implicated in tumorigenesis." Little Caitlin stopped speaking. She could tell by the doctor's expression he was kind of going into shock. She was trying to speak to the doctor in the simplest form that he would understand.

"Das kann nicht wahr sein!" The doctor almost yelled out. Then in English he said, "This can't be true. It can't be happening! If this is some kind of joke it is a whopper!"

"Es ist kein Witz Doktor." Little Kirsten answered in German. "I know this is quite the shock and I do want to talk with you some more but I have ... we have," little Caitlin looked at her parents, "a bit of a problem."

The doctor looked somewhat dumbfounded at the situation and then said, "So you expect me to believe you are some kind of genius?"

"Ask me any question you want to? Any question?" Little Kirsten or rather Caitlin fired back.

"Okay … I'll play along." The doctor said with a smirk. "Any question huh?" He took out his calculator and punched in some numbers and then asked, "What is 136 times … " but before he asked the entire question the little girl blurted out the answer, which was "116,416."

"Egads! I was going to ask what 136 times 856 equaled and you gave the answer before I asked or rather finished the question. Who are you?" The doctor was really in shock now. "And how did you do that?"

"I am just a little girl who just happens to be pretty smart. Now please listen. We have some people … Government Agents from the United States that are trying to capture me and Mommy and Daddy because of my intelligence. We haven't done anything wrong but they really want me … for my intelligence. They are a few hours behind us and in Paris right now searching for us. I singled you out because of not just the stem cell work you and your colleagues are doing but because of the past Dr. Froehlich."

"My past?" The doctor queried back.

"Yes … please bare with me. By the past I mean the past of your father and grandfather … the Holocaust … and the Gestapo. I know about that and I got the sense that you don't like authority … especially when it is governmental or especially if it is like a persecution. We do not want an internment by the government." Caitlin was looking at Dr. Froehlich.

"You know about my father and grandfather and what happened? But how is that possible. I never talk about that. Ever! It is just too terrible! How do you know about that?" The doctor was feeling like his head might explode with an overload of information … shocking information.

"It is difficult to explicate to you how I know. I just felt it in a way but it is more than that. We are asking for your help though. I hadn't planned it until just a short time ago but this is better than the original plan because now I can help you with your stem cell work as well. Not right now but perhaps I could send you something. You need to know that some government agents will be questioning you about me. They are going to question passengers on the train."

"Kirsten … you can stop right there … if that is even your real name? I understand completely now and I am shocked but I must tell you this is … this meeting is the best thing that ever has happened to me … besides the birth of my two children and meeting and marrying my wife. I really believe that. During the war there were good people that helped some of my family escape the Gestapo. My Grandfather didn't survive Auschwitz but my Dad did. He told me some of it. He didn't really like to talk about it much. I have a good feeling about you. I have a car …" but the doctor never got to finish.

"Exactly what I was thinking Sir." Caitlin turned smiling at Mommy and Daddy who were shocked as well. It seemed they were both shocked daily by this little girl who just happened to be their loving daughter.

"Oh no!" The doctor suddenly remembered the cameras in the train had been recording them but before he could say anything further he was interrupted again.

"It's okay. You don't have to worry about the cameras. I have taken care of that." She flashed her cutest smile.

The doctor just stared back at the little girl and the parents. "You've taken care of that? You mean the cameras?"

"Yes … I meant the cameras. They aren't working."

"Oh … well … that's good? But how?" He just had to ask.

"Don't ask." The mother looked at the doctor "You wouldn't believe it anyway. She is quite the little girl wouldn't you say doctor."

The doctor just gave a quizzical look and nodded his head in agreement. "Yes … she certainly is amazing … a miracle of God I would dare say."

"You and I and Mommy and Daddy are going to be great friends doctor." Caitlin's beautiful eyes were looking at the doctor. "I just know it."

The doctor just stared at the little girl … the same kind of look as when he witnessed the birth of his son and daughter. Only this was the birth of something different … something wondrous that had never before been revealed to mankind.

CHAPTER 11

HUNTED: TRACKING PREY

James 4:14
*"Why, you do not even know what will happen tomorrow. What is your
life? You are a mist that appears for a little while and then vanishes."*

The N.S.A. team and the French Authorities raced off as fast as they could to the train station. They felt they were getting closer and their instincts were to turn the heat up and make sure their prey knew there would be no escape. In a sense the gauntlet would be laid and it was only a matter of time before the noose would tighten on the prey.

Agent Baxter rode with her supervisor O'Reilly and she was thinking quite a lot about this family. The family had been off their radar before all these strange intrusions into the N.S.A. computer systems. There was nothing to suspect them of before but red flags started suddenly appearing. She started to ask herself how did they manage to shutdown the power so the cameras would not capture their faces or their movements? Did they work for someone or some other group that was an enemy to the United States? And how did they elude the agents so effectively? The N.S.A. team had never been so misdirected before ... especially when they were so certain to capture their suspects? And how did they make it seem they were on that jet going to Berlin when they never boarded? What really was bothering Baxter the most though was the image of that little girl on the computer working on the Math that no one could understand? I mean there were some very smart people working at the N.S.A. and these so-called experts in their various fields hadn't seen anything like it. So advanced. In Baxter's mind it was almost futuristic in nature. She couldn't wait to get to the train station at the airport. Then she started thinking was this yet another trick? Was this yet another misdirection to send the team off on a wild goose chase?

Agent Baxter needed to say something to her boss. "Sir ... I've been thinking about Berlin."

"What about Berlin," O'Reilly shot back. "That was a total waste of our time. There is going to be hell to pay by someone for that mistake."

"Well ... Sir ... that's what I've been thinking about. It wasn't a mistake ... at least not by the suspects. The various trips they set up ... the counterfeit passports and I.D. they used … they were all designed to send us off in the wrong direction. So now I am just wondering if the Paris Train Station is another misdirection?" Baxter paused to judge the response to what she was suggesting.

"Continue Baxter." O'Reilly said while looking at her.

"Well … it might be wise considering what happened in Berlin to make certain they are on the train. I am wondering if the suspects might use misdirection again and either board a jet bound for some other Country … or even travel by car or some other mode of transportation to some other destination. I don't think they would use a car, as one would think it reasonable that they would want to get as far away from pursuit as quickly as possible. You mentioned the possibility earlier about them boarding a jet but we need to be certain where they went. We should double check the airlines for other flights just to verify that they didn't fly out? We should not dismiss the idea that they have other counterfeit I.D. either."

"That makes sense Baxter. I have to admit that was a pretty elaborate plan of escape that sent us off to Berlin." O'Reilly eyes seemed to squint.

Agent Baxter was looking at O'Reilly as he spoke and she noticed or rather thought he had an almost evil look in his eyes. This time though there was no peering over the coffee cup.

"I'm going to report to the office and give them an update and see if they have any more Intel for us." O'Reilly told Baxter and Sandford. He called the office back in the United States and in no time was speaking to his superior Weatherly. "Sir … the suspects have definitely left the Hotel. We believe they left the hotel to go to the train station. That is where we are headed now. The French Authorities and the D.G.S.I. are escorting us to the train station. We are checking all leads … including the possibility that they boarded another jet."

"Do you know when the suspects left the hotel O'Reilly?"

"We believe it was this morning Sir so they are several hours ahead of us. If they took the train and the French Inspector and I were thinking they are possibly heading for Switzerland … we will take the Military jet and that should shorten the time gap between us." O'Reilly said in a very official voice.

"Very well. Keep us informed. Have you contacted the Swiss authorities yet to be on the lookout for the suspects?" Weatherly asked.

"Well … no Sir … not yet. We are still trying to ascertain if the suspects travelled to Switzerland?"

"O'Reilly … you know this is a very important mission and capture. There is a lot at stake here … the safety and security of our Country. You should have notified the Swiss of the possibility as soon as you thought the suspects might travel there. How long have you suspected they boarded the train to Switzerland?" Weatherly demanded to know.

"Not long Sir … maybe about 20 minutes ago when we found out about the train station … 30 minutes tops." O'Reilly was trying to minimize the possible mistake.

"So that is 30 minutes lost that the Swiss could have been mobilized and searching for the suspects. Geez! Get on the ball O'Reilly! We will notify the Swiss that the suspects are thought to have boarded a train into their Country a few hours ago. We need to use our allies and their resources to aid in the capture of the suspects." Weatherly was obviously pissed off.

"Yes Sir." O'Reilly answered. Baxter could see O'Reilly's face had become a flush red as well as his front neck area. She had never before heard O'Reilly being well … reprimanded like that.

Then Weatherly continued, "O'Reilly ... I also want to tell you that our Red Team ... the best I.T.'s have been going over the seized computer from the home. They've spent a lot of hours trying to access it without success. From what we are being told it is really a complicated firewall that has been set up. Not like anything we have every seen before. It is some kind of program that rewrites the security wall completely about every seven or eight seconds. At least that is what we think? So far we can't even get into the computer to see what the data is at any stage. We also know that somehow they or someone is controlling our satellite systems. Our satellite coverage has been compromised. We were taking satellite photos over Paris and Berlin but the satellites shutdown for some reason. We were hoping to get some pictures of the suspects. O'Reilly ... this is now a priority level one that you and the team capture those suspects. It is imperative that we discover how they accessed our system, and compromised our security without us even knowing about it. The C.I.A. and the F.B.I. are working with us on this one. Their security systems were compromised also. Find those suspects! Understand! And make sure they are alive! We have notified the President that our National Security has been compromised and is at risk. This is an extremely serious matter!"

"Yes Sir. We are going to get them Sir. I will notify the team immediately Sir."

"Let us know when your team arrives in Switzerland O'Reilly." Then he said a curt, "That is all," and hung up.

O'Reilly looked at Baxter and she could tell he was feeling the pressure from above. She could feel it too!

"Serious stuff Sir but we are gonna get them." Baxter said in a consoling manner.

"Damn right we are going to get them Baxter! Enough of this bullshit! One would think that a father, and the mother of Chinese descent ... and

101

they are travelling with a Child … that should be fairly easy to find … a kind of strange combination like that?" O'Reilly said as he looked for agreement.

"Let's get these bastards Sir." She too had a face of frustration. Nobody was going to make the N.S.A. look like a fool … or make her look like a fool.

As they pulled up to the train station Inspecteur Guerrier exited the vehicle and approached O'Reilly. "Hey O'Reilly … good news. We have tracked down and talked with the taxi driver who picked up the family at the Hotel this morning and he did drive them to this train station. They arrived at 8:16 A.M. He remembers them very clearly … not only because the family is a bit of an odd mix with the Chinese woman and the Caucasian man but especially because of the Child. The taxi driver said he especially remembers the little girl. He said she seemed to be very smart for such a little girl. He doesn't know where they were going though. He said the little girl was speaking a foreign language … Chinese or Japanese or something. He wasn't sure."

"Probably Chinese as the mother is Chinese." O'Reilly stated.

The team moved quickly to the train station and it wasn't long before they confirmed the family bought tickets to Zurich. O'Reilly called the Military pilots to get the jet ready for departure immediately. They were leaving for Zurich and would be there in no time. Before they left O'Reilly informed Inspecteur Guerrier that the N.S.A. team were leaving for Switzerland A.S.A.P.

"I want to thank you Inspector Guerrier … and your team and to thank France on behalf of the United States of America. You and your team have been very helpful." O'Reilly tried to make it sound sincere. He wasn't very good at it … making it sound sincere. He got along better with the French than the Germans. At least that is what Baxter thought?

"Good luck O'Reilly. Please let us know how you make out and if we can be of any further assistance do not hesitate to ask. We will continue our investigation to gather any more information." But the N.S.A. team was already off to the waiting Military jet. They would be landing in Zurich within the hour.

CHAPTER 12

CROSSING BORDERS: SHADOWS AND PHANTOMS

Leviticus 26:6

"'I will grant peace in the land, and you will lie down and no one will make you afraid. I will remove wild beasts from the land, and the sword will not pass through your country."

At the Zurich Train Station in Switzerland the Swiss Authorities were already looking for the suspects. They left as soon as the request came in from the National Security Agency. A Levin Ottinger from the Federal Intelligence Service (F.I.S.) in Switzerland was at the Zurich train station with his team. They also had with them the local Cantonal Police Force. They were to search and find the family of three that were believed to be on the train coming into Zurich. There was a Caucasian male about thirty years old, a female of Chinese descent also about thirty years old, and a Child of mixed descent about four to five years old and likely to be holding a rag doll. The Swiss authorities were informed that the suspects might be using the names "Gray" or "Brennan" but likely would be using counterfeit passports and identification papers under some other name. The suspects were designated as high priority targets.

The relationship between the Swiss Federal Intelligence Service and the United States National Security Agency was strained, just as it was with Germany and a few other nations because a few years earlier there was the scandal that America was spying on it's so-called allies. Both sides had attempted to put those scandals behind them but that was not an easy thing to do.

It was obvious to Ottinger from what he knew that the train the suspects were supposed to be on had arrived in Zurich some four hours earlier. The suspects had that much of a head start. They had started their protocol searches when they got word the N.S.A. Military jet had arrived and the N.S.A. team would be along shortly. Thus begun a wide sweeping search of local airports, taxi, bus, rental car services, etc., to ascertain if the suspects could be located. The various spy agencies and police worked together to find the suspects. They also had a list of passengers on the train that they wished to speak with to see if they could extract any information regarding the suspects. This would all take some time but with luck the suspects were still in the area. After two days of searching and interviewing the passengers on the train the trail had ended.

The one passenger on the train that had been seen talking to the family and the little girl with the rag doll had disappeared as well.

⌒⫟⌒

On a beautiful secluded beach far away a little girl in bare feet walked in the sand along the shoreline with her Mommy and Daddy. From the Villa Dr. Froehlich watched his guests. The Villa belonged to a good friend of his. He had called his friend to explain that there was an emergency and that it was all supposed to be hush-hush. That he would explain to his good friend later but he needed a place to hide out for just a few days. His good friend of many years did not hesitate in providing the Villa for use.

"This feels so good Mommy and Daddy doesn't it? I love the way the sand and water feels on my toes. This is way better than those California beaches." Little Caitlin noticed that Mommy and Daddy were holding hands as they walked and she was happy. She was happy for the first time in a while. She felt her parents were safe.

"It is so lovely here Caitlin. What beautiful scenery. It is spectacular here. I would love to live here and stay forever." The Mommy cooed to her daughter and husband.

"It is an amazing place and I have my two favorite girls here by my side. How could I ask for more?" The Daddy looked at his wife and daughter and then at the blue water.

"I would love to stay here too Mommy but we can only stay for three more days."

Little Caitlin sighed when she said it.

Both parents stopped walking and looked at their little girl.

"Look Mommy and Daddy. See our footprints in the sand and how they disappear when the waves come." Little Caitlin watched her tiny footprints and Mommy and Daddy's footprints as they were lapped away by the water and then they were gone. Gone forever it seemed. Which was symbolic to her and her parents. "Right now the bad people can't find our footprints. We are like the sand and the waves but that will change. And so we will need to leave this place. But from now on we will leave few footprints for them to follow."

Little Caitlin looked back at the Villa and Dr. Froehlich was no longer watching them.

Caitlin called to her parents, "Mommy ... Daddy ... come over here and stand by me. I want to show you something."

The Mommy and Daddy went over and stood by their daughter. They stood about ten feet from the small waves gently caressing just where the wet sand met the dry sand. Little Caitlin was looking out to the water ... her little eyes searching.

"What are you looking at Caitlin? Do you see something out there?" The father asked.

The little girl reached out and then she was holding both their hands. She looked up at them, smiled and simply said, "Watch." The little girl looked out at the water as the waves were gently rolling in. And then suddenly the waves stopped. By stopped I mean the water didn't become calm but rather the waves just stopped. Like it was a photograph ... each wave cresting and in essence frozen in time. Little Caitlin looked up at her parents and they were staring at the sea and the waves like they were looking at a postcard.

"I've been practicing Mommy and Daddy and now I can freeze time for a much longer period. I have frozen the whole beach area ... the people, birds, fish, and well everything encompassed in it. See the two birds off to the left farther down in the sky. They are … frozen. Not frozen temperature wise but frozen in time."

Twenty seconds had passed when the father said, "Unfreeze them Caitlin? Does that hurt them?"

Caitlin unfroze time and then said, "No … it doesn't hurt them and they don't even know they were frozen."

"How do you do that honey?" The Daddy asked. He and Mommy were stunned. She told them she had done it before but this time they actually witnessed it in person.

"I'm not sure Daddy. I just think about it and it happens. Like when you think and decide to pick up a pen. Something like that is how I can explain it. And I control the molecules but now I can control the atoms and even more. Look at the water again but don't be afraid. Watch."

Little Caitlin was still holding onto Mommy and Daddy's hands and looking out at the sea. Then the parents noticed a wall of water being built about three hundred feet from shore but the wall wasn't moving that they could tell. It just kept building and building … getting taller and taller until it was about fifty feet tall. And then the little girl released it and the giant wall of water was rushing towards the beach where they were standing. It was a tidal wave. Both parents held their daughter's hands tighter.

Little Caitlin said, "Don't be afraid. It's okay."

And then when the wave was about one hundred feet from the beach it just suddenly stopped dead in its tracks and then slowly decreased in size until it was gone. It was like it never existed. It was like an ice cube that had melted quickly. And then only small waves lapped at the grains of sand on the shore … just as they had before the demonstration.

"My God! If I didn't see it I would never believe it." The father blurted out in shock.

The mother didn't quite know what to say. She just stared at her little girl. The mother was afraid. Being smart was one thing but being able to control waves and time was something else.

"I've been experimenting ... testing things out Mommy and Daddy. I need to prepare for the future and I need to know how to protect you ... and how to protect me too!" Caitlin tried to explain. The concept of time is special and I have more to learn but I am finding I can do more things every day. It makes me feel ... safer."

"Are you afraid Caitlin?" Daddy asked his little girl.

Caitlin gave a half smile that showed her apprehension. "Right now there are only two things that scare me."

"What are the two things that scare you honey?" Mother asked ... her face showing the combination of concern and shock.

"I'm afraid for you Mommy and Daddy and what those bad people might try to do but even more I am afraid of what I could do to them ... all of them ... if they tried to hurt you. I don't want to hurt anyone but if they hurt you or Daddy ... I am not sure what I would do?" Her little face showed anger again ... the same type of anger that she showed in the jet a few days earlier. Although she seemed very wise she was still just a very young Child. "That is what scares me the most. What could happen? I am capable of great destruction but I am also capable of great things ... even now. And it is funny that I can control time ... or parts of it ... yet I have to wait for the evolution of my brain and abilities to develop further."

Both parents looked down at their little girl. Such innocence was mixed with the realization that there existed real evil in the World and that things were not fair in life. For Caitlin she believed in the morality and ethics her parents had taught her since she was but seven days old. There was a conflict building inside her though. That conflict might one day be her greatest battle.

"I want you to promise you won't hurt people Caitlin." Mommy stated looking down at her little daughter. "That is very important. Otherwise you are just like them. Promise you won't hurt them."

"Yes Caitlin, always remember to avoid violence and anger. Anger is the enemy of the soul." The father added.

The little girl looked up at her parents and then asked some questions but in her heart she knew they didn't really know the answers. "Why are there wars Mommy and Daddy? Why is there racism Mommy and Daddy? Why is there poverty and sickness when it could be wiped out? Why do people prefer greed to kindness? I have much to think about? I am still learning and I am learning many things. I will try to control my anger Daddy. I will promise you that. And I will try not to hurt anyone but that is all I can promise the both of you. For now we are safe. We should enjoy this time." Little Caitlin looked out to the scene of the beautiful sea and smiled. "Now let's go in and see Dr. Froehlich. I want to work on the computer and later give it to him. I have much to give this good man that will help in his stem cell research. I won't be needing a computer anymore … I have this." Little Caitlin pointed to her brain.

"What do you mean by that Caitlin?" Daddy asked

"I mean I can now connect to the World wide-web or other computers better than a computer can with just my brain. I have my own Wi-Fi in a sense although it is much more advanced and secure. I thought about it last night and then tried it and it worked." Caitlin tried her best to explain the unexplainable.

"Oh my?" Mommy responded and looked at her husband. "Well … I guess we won't need to buy anymore computers for her."

There was a silence and then the three of them walked across the white sands of the beach to the Villa. The Villa itself was splendid; a beautiful architecture with an open balcony at floor level leading to the beach. Around much of the Villa were many beautiful flowers. The Tuscany poppies, the Dahlias, the Orchids, the Peonies … also called the "Rose without thorns." There were rose bushes consisting of bright blood red and virgin white roses about the Villa. Above on the second floor was a beautiful balcony with a splendid view facing the sea as well. Inside the Villa the furniture was exquisite. A grandiose place that showed the opulence of a different life style. A grand piano in a main room, paintings hung on the wall and richness abounded. Inside the doctor sat at the comfy chair reading. His life had been good to him. He had money himself and didn't need to work but he wanted to. There was the need to do something great bred into him … and of course to help his beloved wife who was sick in the nursing home.

Little Caitlin entered the room and smiled at seeing him and ran to him. She surprised him with a big hug and a kiss and said to him, "I really like this place. You feel like a grandfather to me Dr. Froehlich. Would it be okay to call you Grandpapa?"

The doctor smiled and looked at the parents who were smiling too! "And you are like a grand-daughter to me Caitlin."

The little girl turned to Mommy and Daddy and asked, "You don't mind do you Mommy and Daddy?"

Mommy and Daddy looked at each other and kind of made an "Oh … why not kind of face to each other." Daddy said, "Ah … I guess that would be okay Caitlin?"

"Okay then … it's settled! I will call you Grandpapa. Mommy and Daddy … you stay with Grandpapa and talk with him. Answer any questions he may have. You can trust him completely. I am going to work on the computer for a couple of hours. Okay?" Then little Caitlin turned to look back at her new Grandpapa and said, "And I am going to give you something that will help with your wife's Alzheimer's disease. Bye for now."

The doctor was astounded. He was without words after hearing that this little girl … this almost stranger of intelligence somehow knew his wife had Alzheimer's disease and it was as if he had been hit by a lightning bolt! It was as if she could read his mind but that wasn't possible? How did she know about his wife? He had never mentioned his wife's condition before? And how did she know the answer to that math question before he even asked it? Little Caitlin turned and ran into to the other room and sat in a chair. From there she could see the group and do her work on the laptop.

The doctor had no real idea what the little girl was about to give him … much more than just the eventual Alzheimer's cure. He was in such shock at what she had just said. He was well aware that this little girl had a very special intelligence. The time they spent in the car from Zurich to Genoa, although only a bit over four hours confirmed in his mind that this was one very special person. He was simply amazed. She told him her real name and he had never met anyone filled with such knowledge about so many things. He realized something very quickly during that car ride. That this little girl was smarter than he was … even in his specialty field … and by a lot. Someone very great sat in that car with him and she wasn't even five years old yet? It was scary in a way but the possibilities excited him. Overwhelming really.

The mother and father sat down in chairs close to the doctor. The doctor admitted to the parents, "That is one incredibly smart little girl you have there. Where does she get such super intelligence? Do you know?"

The father answered, "I don't really know where it comes from? She is on a level of intelligence far beyond any human being that has ever lived. We are sure of that. It must be innate or some kind of genetic influence? She started speaking at seven days old and it just grew from there."

"Seven days old?? You mean she said her first word at only seven days old? That is simply amazing." The doctor murmured at being told.

The mother added, "It wasn't that she said her first word at seven days old but she actually just started speaking sentences. At seven days old she shocked both of us when she started conversing with us. There was no warning or sign ahead of that. It was just suddenly there?"

"My God? And what did she say?" The doctor asked. "I am most curious?"

Both father and mother started to laugh. The mother smiled as she answered. "Well ... believe it or not she told us she wanted to watch the television. She said I want to watch the television. That's a direct quote."

"I want to watch the television?" The doctor repeated in a higher pitched voice. Then he too laughed. Then he said, "No other human has ever talked so early. Not since the beginning of time I imagine. Has she ever taken an I.Q. test?"

"There's really no point doctor. I really believe she was too smart for any such test some time ago." The father responded. There was a slight silence as the doctor was thinking what to ask next? Then the father added, "Caitlin completed University studies at just a few months old. Not that she had been to a University you see but she was studying and learning at incredible rates. Her math ... I don't understand it? I haven't been able to understand her Math for years now. And I thought I was pretty good at Math but this is beyond me ... or anyone else for that matter. She tried to explain it to me but I was lost ... just like my wife was lost trying to figure out the math and she is a math expert. Caitlin is working on the computer especially for you now. She never saves anything on the computer as she just remembers it. She has no need to save it but now she is going to save it on the computer for you."

"I am …how do Americans say it? Totally blown away by all this."

The parents laughed. "I will tell you that since the seventh day and from that day on we were and are totally blown away every day by our little girl." The mother said it with a certain pride.

"Well … you are welcome to stay here for a couple of months if you want. I have worked that out with my friend. I can only stay a few more days though. I have to get back to my family and work in Switzerland."

"We know Dr. Froehlich. Only three more days … am I right? Father was smiling at the doctor as he looked at him.

"Why yes … I must leave in three more days but how did you know?"

"Well … Caitlin told us when we had to leave so we figured that is when you were leaving?" Father answered.

"But how would she know? I never said as much?" The doctor said looking quite puzzled yet again. "She seems to know things before being told … like she's psychic?"

"I don't know how she knows things and she seems to know things no one else does." The mother responded.

"Hmmm … amazing. Seeing as we are going to be here together for a few days why don't you call me by my first name … Lucas. I would prefer that."

"All right Lucas. Thank you … and you know I am Michael and this is Nuwa."

"Michael … you said earlier on the ride that you are a Neurobiologist and Nuwa is a neuroscientist. We work in almost the same type of fields to each other and so our work has a similarity to it. Perhaps that is how your daughter knows so much about stem cell research? I wonder?" Lucas queried.

Michael responded, "Lucas … I can tell you without any doubt that my daughter's knowledge in the subject surpassed that of myself … or Nuwa's work some time ago … years ago in fact. What we know compared to her is minuscule. Really quite depressing in a way when you think of it. Caitlin wants to talk with you after she is finished on the computer. We should warn you though that these next few days are not only going to shock you even further but we think you are going to have some totally new insights into stem cell research."

Lucas sat in silence for a few seconds then added, "You know … this … all this is in itself a difficult concept to grasp … so much intelligence." Lucas shook his head in disbelief. "And so young. It seems so impossible yet there it is … I mean there she is." Lucas continued shaking his head ever so slightly just like someone does when they see something they simply don't understand or can't believe what has happened.

"That's not all Lucas," the mother interjected, "her intelligence … her abilities are growing daily. And Michael and I have no idea when it will stop or even if it will stop. It is a bit scary. That is why the government is after us. They have no idea how smart she really is or the extent of her intelligence but they are beginning to and that is scary too!"

"Well … you are safe here and your secret I will take to my grave. I won't even tell my Children or my wife." Lucas reassured although his wife's current stage of Alzheimer's was more towards the advanced stages. She had some good days but they were rare. Lucas had some sadness in his eyes when he mentioned his wife and the parents noticed it. They talked for two hours non-stop getting to know each other better. There was no shortage of words or questions.

CHAPTER 13

AN ODYSSEY OF WONDER: CONFESSIONS

Proverbs 18:15
"An intelligent heart acquires knowledge, and the ear of the wise seeks knowledge."

After two hours of diligently working on the computer little Caitlin was done. She had included her own security systems into this computer and they were far beyond any current available security systems. She had built in multiple walls of what she termed "Cloaking Devices" and each with a higher level of encryption and security of the data. And just like the first computer ... anyone attempting to break in would be met with an ever-changing firewall ... although the term firewall was inappropriate. It was more like an Atom Fusion Wall of protection. Or in other words ... virtually unbreakable ... except by her.

The little girl called out to the next room, "Grandpapa ... Mommy ... Daddy ... come here please. I'm ready!"

All three turned their heads to look over at Caitlin as she smiled at them and waved for them to come in.

"This is going to be interesting." The father stated to Lucas. "Do you want to take a drink first? I think you might be needing it." The father and mother laughed at the comment.

"You know ... I think I will take your advice. In fact ... perhaps we should all have a little drink ... don't you think?"

And so Lucas opened a bottle of 1990 Chateau Latour. This was after all a very special occasion. Lucas poured three glasses of the wine and they each took a sip.

"Wow! This is pretty good wine Lucas. It tastes great! How much does a bottle of this stuff cost?" The father asked as he took another small sip.

"It is over a thousand dollars a bottle. So your wine glass is holding about two hundred dollars of the stuff. The more expensive wines we keep in the wine cellar." Lucas smiled back.

"Oh ... gee ... I better not spill any then huh?" The father held up the wine glass to the light inspecting it like he might find a diamond or ruby in the bottom of the glass.

Mother laughed and whispered to him, "I guess when you own a Villa price doesn't matter so much?"

"Hey ... what's taking so long?" Little Caitlin yelled out as she strained her neck trying to see what they were doing. "I'm waaaiiting."

"We're coming honey." The Mommy answered.

"Pull up some chairs so you can see." Little Caitlin ordered the adults.

They all pulled up a chair and looked at the monitor. The first thing the little girl explained was how important it was to remember how to access this computer.

"And Grandpapa ... you can't write this stuff down. It must be in your head. If anyone else gets this information they can access it and it is important that doesn't happen. Do you understand?"

"Uh ... okay?" Grandpapa felt funny taking instructions from a little girl.

"Don't worry though. I will go over it with you many times over the next few days. Don't write the data down anywhere else and keep the laptop in some place safe. No notepads or other recordings. I suggest you release the information in stages to your colleagues Grandpapa." Little Caitlin looked at him as she was speaking. "I've also backed it up with a retinal recognition program through the webcam should you need to access it a second way. It coincides with a voice recognition system and I will set up both. I want you to switch chairs with me Grandpapa." They switched chairs and little Caitlin asked Grandpapa to lean forward and look at the webcam and speak into the computer and repeat clearly three times the word "Starlight." As he did that little Caitlin watched and listened. "Okay … now let's test it." She shut the system down and asked him to start the computer. They tested it and the visual and voice recognition worked. She also showed him another way to access the computer without the voice or retinal displays. "Okay … I tried my best to make the lessons and data fairly simple. Sorry for saying that but it is very simple to me. Okay … let's start. I will only go over the first part. There are ten parts in total though. I want you to navigate but only when I say to. They are in a specific order so you shouldn't skip steps as there is a building of the knowledge base." It was in fact a sequence or a blue print of steps that Lucas could try back at his lab. The father and mother tried to follow along and they kind of got the data. It was awe-inspiring for all three.

"By lesson ten you will realize that you don't always have to use the embryonic cells for regeneration of neurones. And not only will there be regenerations involving what are called pluripotent stem cells, and I know the researchers are working on that now but what I have given you here they won't achieve for about a three to four decades. Now scientists are discovering in the early stages that those designated as region-selective pluripotent stem cells (rsPSCs), can currently be obtained from the mouse embryos and primate pluripotent stem cells, including humans. This means that the genome of human rsPSCs offers advantages for regenerative medicine applications. You already know some of this but I have just pointed you in a slightly different direction." Little Caitlin spoke to the three like this stuff was so easy. "And as you are beginning to realize although you don't really understand yet there are really endless possibilities and potentials for use beyond blood disorders, blood supply, cancers, cartilage damage, diabetes, hearing or vision, heart disease, infertility, lung diseases, multiple sclerosis, muscular dystrophy, organ replacements, Parkinson's, platelet transfusions, spinal cord injuries, tissue damage … well … really the list is endless since most life forms are cellular in some regard. You and the World will have do come to terms with your own ethical concerns when you reach those levels."

"Oh my God! Oh my God! I am … I don't think there is even a word for it … numb … shocked … I must be dreaming? Caitlin … this is amazing but how do you know it works?" Grandpapa asked. He stared at the screen … thinking … trying to take it in but the more he looked at it … the more it kind of started to make sense … not that he really understood it … at least not quite yet.

"Wow Caitlin! Wow! I had no idea you even knew this kind of stuff. But how do you know it? You haven't been doing any research on stem cells … or have you?" The Mommy asked. Everyone was staring at the little girl in utter shock.

"Not research really but I just worked it out in my head. Once again I don't fully understand how I know it … I just do. And Grandpapa … you asked if I know it works. Well I can tell you it does work on other life forms. I understand the life forms of many creatures … right down to their cellular levels. Mankind will one day discover that there really is only one type of cell for all living things but that there are many variations that cells may take. All diseases and sicknesses cannot only be treated but also cured and prevented. Even when the disease mutates as it tries to survive. Much like the common cold has done even though that is a simple virus. The race is to catch up to the diseases before they mutate to some other form." The little girl looked at the group and she could tell they were astounded.

So for the next four hours Lucas … or rather the new Grandpapa mulled over lesson one. It was going to take years to go over all ten lessons. Caitlin left him alone to look at it. And over the next couple of days they would talk a lot. He had many questions and there was only one place on the planet he could get the answers. And it was in the form of a four and a half year old girl that walked the planet.

⌒⌒⌒

Meanwhile in Zurich the officials were still interviewing witnesses on the train and searching for the suspects. There were no leads as to what happened to the suspects? And the big mystery was where was the man, a Dr. Lucas Froehlich that was on the train and was seen talking with the suspects for about three hours? Where did he go? It was as if they all had vanished? The agents talked with the doctor's two Children but they had no idea where he was and they seemed quite worried as to his whereabouts as well. The wife had Alzheimer's and so talking to her was a complete waste of time but the teams were not leaving any stone unturned. They contacted the doctor's colleagues at work, his friends and even talked to his supposed best friend but with no luck. The F.I.S. got the phone records to see if there was any trace ... any clues as to what might have happened? There was one call that came to the doctor's best friend's house on the day the train arrived in Zurich. The call was from a throw away phone that was untraceable and the phone call was only 38 seconds long. Some know it as a "Burner" phone. A phone that when purchased isn't registered and is used for an extra level of privacy. They wondered who made that call and what was the conversation about? The doctor's friend, a Dr. Goldman, was a rich well-respected businessman. Dr. Goldman would tell the F.I.S. he didn't really remember the call but thought it was a wrong number?

The Villa was actually owned by a friend of Dr. Goldman. The F.I.S. agents and the N.S.A. agents kept looking ... searching for a lead but nothing was there. The Cantonal Police Force seemed to be not having any luck either. The cameras were not functioning in the train that the suspects were in and it seemed that as the suspects moved about the cameras monitoring those areas would suddenly shutdown. It happened at the airports, the taxis, the hotel, the train station, the train, the various satellites ... and well ... everywhere.

O'Reilly mentioned it to Ottinger. "Have you ever heard or are you aware of some kind of jamming device that can shutdown the recording cameras on the train? He did not mention about the satellites being compromised."

"The suspects must have a jamming device rendering the electronics ... the cameras that is ... useless ... much like a Stinger." Ottinger had a questioning look on his face. "They are obviously aware they are being pursued and the fact that they have covered their trail so well must mean that they are getting some help. I think Dr. Froehlich either helped them or perhaps the family kidnapped the doctor? Maybe he is a hostage? We have checked and he has a vehicle and that vehicle is missing. We are searching for the vehicle now. We have identified the vehicle ... a new Tungsten Silver Metallic Volkswagen Touareg Execline with license number AG - 12054." Ottinger was looking at O'Reilly ... then over to Agent Baxter as he spoke.

"There must be somebody around them that took a picture with them in it? We haven't been able to find any real pictures of them either which is very unusual?" O'Reilly was looking at Baxter as if his mind was wondering ... thinking.

"You'll get a picture. Someone has a picture. What about the license bureau? They would have pictures as required by law." Ottinger stated.

"That's a negative. They seem to have been wiped clean too! We need to find that vehicle Ottinger ... and Dr. Froehlich ... and check people's cameras that were travelling on the train." O'Reilly was starting to get angry again just thinking about it. How frustrating it was to be always two steps behind? They were closing the gap up until now. Now time was slipping away again and the suspects ... the fugitives could be getting further and further away.

Back at the gorgeous Villa the family were enjoying the break. It was a beautiful place that had privacy, solitude, and was surrounded by the beauty of nature. Little Caitlin spent hours talking with the new Grandpapa about many things but mostly about stem cells and each of the lessons. As far as the doctor or rather Grandpapa knew the little girl was an incredible genius but nothing more. He did not know about her special abilities like her parents did except she seemed able to read minds? Little Caitlin had told her parents that there was no need for him to know and it was better not to tell anyone else about her other very special abilities. If word got out the family would be even more of a target. For now, the United States did not know or have any true idea about the little girl's intelligence. They knew she was intelligent … very smart but they were very much in the dark. There were so many unanswered questions about this little girl and in some respects even the parents had no idea the level of intelligence of their little daughter. In that sense they were in the dark too! How could anyone even begin to comprehend such intelligence? The stem cell knowledge was only the surface of her knowledge.

On the afternoon before the day of departure from the Villa the parents and Caitlin were out on the ground level balcony looking out at a luxury yacht in the calm sea off in the distance. It was quite far off and the parents were using a telescope set up on the lower patio to view the yacht.

"Come look at this yacht Caitlin." The Mommy cooed to her daughter. "The person who owns that must be some rich billionaire or something?"

"That's okay. I can see it just fine Mommy."

"You really should take a look honey. You will get a much better view using the telescope." The Daddy chirped in.

"No I won't Daddy. I see better without the telescope." Caitlin kind of whispered as she looked around to make sure Grandpapa wasn't within earshot. He was off in the other room devouring the stem cell data Caitlin had left him on the computer.

Daddy and Mommy looked at Caitlin. Then Daddy asked, "What do you mean you see better without the telescope?"

Little Caitlin looked at Daddy … then at Mommy and there was a slight pause. She decided to tell them. "My eyes are not exactly like your eyes. A normal person sees 20/20 and that is called perfect vision but my eyes have become enhanced … as well as my other senses." Caitlin paused and both Mommy and Daddy were … just looking at her with that deer in the headlights kind of look.

"What do you mean by enhanced Caitlin?" Mommy asked and both waited for a response.

"Well … my eyes have telephoto abilities. In fact far beyond that telescope you have there. I can focus on things far away and beyond the capabilities of a telescope. For example Daddy … look at the boat at the bow where the anchor is. Do you see the name of the boat? I can see it quite clearly. The name is Wandering Gypsy."

The Daddy looked in the telescope and found it. Then Mommy looked in the telescope to see it. They had to put the telescope on its most powerful setting to see it.

"You can see way out there with just your eyes Caitlin?" Daddy asked.

"I can see farther than that … much farther." Caitlin answered. "Okay … I might was well tell you the rest. Daddy … Mommy … I also have night vision. I can see in total darkness. Better than any I.R.V. or N.V.D. system. I can also look at the sun without hurting my eyes. I have a natural filter for that. The U.V. application comes in handy for that. You have to be careful or it will damage your eyes." She didn't need to warn them though. Everyone knows don't look at the sun without proper protection.

"Good God Caitlin! How far can you see? And you have night vision and you can look at the sun?" Daddy sat down in the chair beside him. He was looking at his wife and then would just stare at his daughter. "So you are kind of like Superman … or rather Supergirl … aren't you?"

Caitlin looked at her Daddy and shook her head, "No Daddy." Then she sighed, "I can't fly or leap over tall buildings and I can't stop a speeding bullet. Oh wait … I can stop a speeding bullet … I think. When I stop time I mean. Physically I am pretty much like most humans but it is my brain that has given me the abilities to do these things."

"Caitlin … how long … how long have you had these … abilities? I mean with your eyes?" Mommy asked.

"Not too long." Little Caitlin wasn't exactly truthful and she felt guilty but she knew if she told her parents for a few years they might be resentful for not being told earlier. "I might as well tell you I also have thermal or heat detection so I could follow heat signatures for tracking of wildlife … or people. And it is sensitive. I checked it out and I can follow heat signatures through people's shoes … for example … and days later their heat prints are still there. I'd be very good at tracking people … or things. I have more to tell you. Are you ready?" Caitlin looked at her parents faces judging how they were taking all this in."

"There's more Caitlin?" The Mommy questioned. "Oh boy."

"No … Oh girl is what you should say Mommy." Little Caitlin smiled. "Yea … actually there is quite a bit more to tell you." Caitlin checked back to see the Grandpapa still working on the computer oblivious to what was being revealed only a few yards away. "I also have x-ray abilities and something quite new. I call it M.D.V. for short."

"What is M.D.V.?" The Daddy was almost afraid to ask.

"I call it Multi-Density Vision? I can detect things that have various densities. For example … I can detect in the dark … or light … different densities of objects or things. So I could detect for example people in a building … behind walls or desks or things like that. I would really suck at hide and go seek cause … well … I see everything easily … it wouldn't be fair." Little Caitlin gave a little giggle at that comment. "That would come in handy for example if I was searching for a dead body with no heat signature or if in total darkness … or light … I could detect things like who was wearing bullet proof vests and such. In that regard the Military or police have no technological advantages on me? And there is more. Do you want to hear it?"

"Please continue. We want to hear more Caitlin." Daddy sighed.

Caitlin looked at Mommy and Daddy and decided she would tell them only a few more things. They looked shocked enough. There would be another time to tell them the other abilities. "Okay then … back to the eyes. My eyes can also act like a microscope all the way down to the electron level … and beyond. I'll be a bit brief. My hearing is ultra sensitive for U.H.L.H. That means Ultra High/Low Hearing. I also have U.A.H., which is Ultra Acute Hearing. So I not only can hear high and low sound waves but I can hear sounds multiplied beyond regular human ears. I could hear whispering a few thousand feet away if I focused for example. I also have V.S.T. or what I call Variable Sensitivity Touch. I mean by that that I can have a very sensitive touch and feel things that regular humans couldn't. But I could also change the sensitivity … if I needed or wanted to pick up a boiling pot of water … or put my hand in a fire for example. And no … my skin wouldn't get burnt or damaged. I tried it with some battery acid … sulphuric acid and it had no effect. I also have H.S.S. or what I call High Sensitivity Smell. I can smell better than a moth can and they have the one of the best sensitivities to smell on the planet. I can also shut it down … my olfactory senses … if need be. Like in case there was a really bad smell." Caitlin then stopped and thought that is all she better tell them for now. That was a lot for them to think about. She didn't tell them she can detect brain wave activity and that she could interpret it as well. She was detecting for example that her parents were reaching the limit in that area. Caitlin smiled and said one last thing. "I know that all this is a shock to you but really when you think of it … all those special abilities sure come in handy evading authorities and will even come in handy should we need to protect ourselves."

They all sat in the open patio but there was a bit of silence after that revelation. "That slight breeze sure feels good huh Mommy and Daddy." She broke the silence as she looked at them … making sure they were all right. She looked right at Daddy for a second and then said, "No Daddy … I can't see through people's clothes."

"Oh my God! You are reading my mind aren't you Caitlin?" The Daddy blurted out. Mommy looked shocked too!

"Remember when Grandpapa was asking me that multiplication question on the train and I told him the answer before he finished asking me the question. Well … I can read people's minds kind of. Not totally but I saw in Daddy's mind that he was thinking about clothes. I also feel things that are transferred. Can't explain it but please don't worry. I am not reading your minds." Little Caitlin tried to calm her parents.

"It's just that … well Caitlin …" But Mommy didn't get to finish.

"I know Mommy. You and Daddy want to have privacy in your thoughts." Caitlin rolled her eyes just a bit.

"Oh my God! Now you read my mind didn't you?" Mommy seemed to panic.

"No Mommy … I didn't read your mind. It just seemed natural and logical that is what you were going to say. That you want me to respect your privacy … and Daddy's privacy of course." Caitlin tried to reassure. "We all have to leave tomorrow and I want to spend some time talking with Grandpapa and to let you know what is next for all of us. You should relax now. We have very little to worry about for quite some time. It will be a nice time for all of us."

"Where are we off to next honey? Mommy asked.

"We have a wonderful adventure ahead of us. It will be a time of great sightseeing and a time to stop worrying … and enjoy a journey of exploration. I know you want to know where we are going and I will tell you tomorrow after Grandpapa leaves. I love you both so much Mommy and Daddy." Caitlin gave each parent a loving hug. Then she said, "I have something to tell Grandpapa."

CHAPTER 14

MEDITERRANEAN MUSIC: MIRACLES

2 Corinthians 11:26
"I have been on frequent journeys, in dangers from rivers, danger from robbers, dangers from my countrymen, dangers from the Gentiles, dangers in the city, dangers in the wilderness, dangers on the sea, dangers among false brethren;"

"Grandpapa! Grandpapa! Can you come here please?" Little Caitlin called out.

Grandpapa pulled himself away from the computer. He had spent a lot of time in front of the computer going over the data and findings Caitlin had revealed to him just a few days earlier. "I'm coming." He closed the laptop and carried his treasure with him into the room where the family was sitting. He was going to miss this little girl, his kind of new adopted granddaughter, and the parents as well. They were good people. He felt that in his heart of hearts.

Grandpapa sat down. It was such a quiet place … a place that seemed to soothe away life's aches and pains. A splendid retreat to all that entered.

"I need to talk to you about tomorrow Grandpapa." Little Caitlin seemed to say in a purring voice. "How do you feel about tomorrow Grandpapa?"

"Well … I feel sad that you are leaving but I am so grateful having met you Caitlin. Are the authorities still looking for me? I would suspect since they want you so badly that they are?"

"Yes … they will question you and I don't want you to get into trouble. You will be stopped at the border when you cross back into Switzerland. I don't want you to lie to them about me but you can't under any circumstances tell them about the stem cell data on the laptop. If you do they will definitely seize it and you will never see it." Caitlin made sure that he understood that. "I suggest you tell them that you came to the Villa and brought us having met us on the train. That you knew nothing that we were wanted fugitives. Just that we struck up a friendship of sorts and you brought us here for a few days to rest. It is important you do not reveal any details about my intelligence or you are going to be interrogated for long periods of time."

"I can do that. They won't get much from me." Grandpapa stated as he looked at his new adopted family.

"You didn't notice anything unusual about us and that we came to talk to you on the train and that we told you we were on vacation but had no real destination. Kind of like an exploration. That you mentioned to us that you were actually going to a friend's Villa in Italy for a few days for a retreat and you asked us if we wanted to come along. If they ask about a Burner phone or a secret phone call you know absolutely nothing about that either. That is important." Caitlin made sure to emphasis that.

"I get it. I will only mention we had a chance meeting ... that you seemed a normal family and I have no idea where you would be going next?" The Grandpapa added.

"Tell them we mentioned we were going to Barcelona. If you mention you have no idea it might seem strange to them or that you are hiding something. Right now they only want to talk to you about us because some passengers on the train noticed we talked. They are going to ask if you have any pictures of us, which you don't. The main point is that you have no idea what is going on or what the fuss is about? You can ask them why they want to talk with us but they won't tell you the truth. They will say that we are of interest and they may even make up some lies about us in order to see how you will react or volunteer information. Be polite but get angry if they are keeping you too long and that you need to get back to work and your family and especially your wife. Do you have any questions for me Grandpapa?"

Grandpapa sighed and he had sadness in his eyes. "Will I ever see or hear from you again Caitlin ... Michael ... Nuwa?"

"Yes you will but not for a couple of years I think. I will find a way. You can be sure of that." Caitlin had sad eyes too! "By the way if you ever really need to contact me ... and I mean because of an emergency of some sort or even questions about the data just make sure your computer is near a wireless and press the help button ten times in about ten seconds. No matter where I am I will get the message. I have arranged it to ping off various satellites that will alert me. The authorities won't be able to track it. Your special group and I don't mean your colleagues but your special group … you know whom I mean … you can tell them about me. I sense that group can be trusted 100%." Caitlin was looking directly into his eyes.

Grandpapa sat in shock! Real shock! No one knew about this special group and yet … somehow she knew but how? It wasn't possible? "How do you … know that … are we talking about the same thing?" Grandpapa looked at the parents but they had no idea what their daughter was talking about. Then he looked back at Caitlin.

She smiled … shrugged her shoulders and answered, "You're group … just tell them … I said hi and for them not to worry about me. Perhaps someday I will meet them … under different circumstances."

They talked for hours, ate supper and talked some more. It was the kind of talk that made everyone more at ease. Then the little girl went over to the Fazioli piano that sat unused at the large window facing the beautiful beach. Although she had never played before she sat at the piano and she played each note separately at first … like she was studying the sound of each note. Then suddenly she began playing Beethoven's Piano Sonata No.14 "Quasi Una Fantasia," Opus and 27, No.2, (Moonlight Sonata) Movement 1: Adagio sostenuto, Movement 2: Allegretto. The three all stared in amazement. How her little hands ever reached all those keys was unknown but they did. And she played the piano as great as any pianist who has ever walked the planet. After the wonder of the miracle there was a moment of silence and then the sound of clapping. All three actually stood up. The little tiny girl turned to them smiling … stood up and then gave a curtsy bow to her audience.

"Why thank you." Caitlin was smiling.

"I had no idea your daughter was an such accomplished pianist? That was absolutely unbelievable! She is pure genius." The Grandpapa exclaimed with enthusiasm.

There was a further silence and then the mother answered, "Neither did we?" She and her husband just stared at each other … then at their little girl.

Then little Caitlin sat back down and played something totally new on the Fazioli. She started to sing as she played but with the voice of what surely had to be an Angel for that is truly what it sounded like. Something never heard before by any person past or present on Earth … and it was so beautiful that the three in the audience had tears in their eyes. That further reaffirmed to Lucas that this little girl that he met only a few days ago had touched not only his mind but also his heart and soul and was really a miracle of God. Not that he needed further reaffirmation of that fact. Lucas was a religious man and although there were times in his life that he questioned his beliefs … his faith … today … now … he wasn't questioning anymore. They all slept as well as could be expected that night. Tomorrow would be a big day.

The next morning everyone was up early at the Villa. Caitlin and Mommy and Daddy and the new Grandpapa all got up early and went out and sat on the sandy white beach to watch the beautiful sunrise together. It was going to be a gorgeous day. While they lay on the beach admiring the sight suddenly four European Turtle Doves landed right in front of the group. It startled everyone except Caitlin. She just smiled at the birds … then at Mommy … Daddy and Grandpapa.

"You know … the European Turtle Dove is mentioned in biblical times in the Song of Songs … a sign that a good omen is coming. The birds are emblems of devoted love. A love for the forever till the end of time." Caitlin said in a very soft voice.

All three stared back and forth at the birds and at Caitlin and the birds stared back at them but mostly they stared at little Caitlin. She held out her tiny hand and all four birds advanced slowly towards her … seemingly with their heads bowed. She ever so gently touched the head of each bird and each bird cooed the dove sound at her touch. Then Caitlin whispered, "These birds have had special meanings over the course of human history." The Mommy reached out her hand to the four birds … touched one of their heads and then the four birds flew up to the sky … circling once … and then flew off to the East towards the rising sun before heading north.

"Did you have anything to do with those birds visiting us Caitlin?" Mommy asked.

All three just stared at Caitlin waiting for her reply. She just smiled back and replied in a soft voice, "Why … whatever do you mean Mommy?" Then she added, "Four birds for the four of us." Then she suddenly exclaimed, "Hey! Just like the four musketeers right? We are the four musketeers." She laughed. Then they all watched and enjoyed the rest of the sunrise but three in the group kept thinking about those four Turtle Doves.

Grandpapa finally spoke. "You know over a thousand of those European Turtle Doves were found dead in the parks and streets in the northern Italian town of Faenza just a couple of years ago. Scientists tried to explain what happened? They said it was a diet change that killed those birds."

Caitlin answered with conviction. "That wasn't exactly true! It has to do with pollution and the environmental issues. The Scientists are finding a great number of deaths and mortality rates of wildlife around the World. Recently there have been lots of birds, fish, whales, dolphins, as well as many honey bees plus many other animals that are dying in great numbers. These are warning signs. I will have to find a better solution if humans have any hope to survive. The Earth is in peril like never before. So many crises on the horizon." Caitlin looked over and she had all three mesmerized so she stopped speaking. "Sorry …

didn't mean to scare you. I'm not sure but I am beginning to think that is why I am here?" Then she continued, "You know ... we all have a choice twice a day to enjoy the sunrises and the sunsets. We all just have to make a conscious decision to notice it ... to see it ... and to take the time to enjoy it. Beauty is all around us in so many different things ... including the people we meet. In a sense the roses are like people. There are thorns that we must watch out for but if we are careful of the thorns and find the petals ... not only do they smell lovely and look lovely but they also feel lovely as well to our touch. Okay ... no more talking. Let us just enjoy the sunrise."

Grandpapa needed to say something. "You know ... you are one amazingly little girl ... and seemingly so wise too? Yet you are only four years old? That is simply incredible ... absolutely incredible. I am amazed beyond words. You certainly don't speak like any four-year old. You are like no one else ... unique beyond compare."

"We are all unique beyond compare Grandpapa ... and I can speak like a four year old if you prefer?" She smirked, "And I am four and a half Grandpapa. You can learn something from everyone ... even when you least expect it. Sometimes grown ups just stop learning. They think they know it all ... ah ... present company excluded of course." She giggled at the last comment.

Hearing a little girl giggle on the beach ... well ... that is a miracle in itself when you think about it. After enjoying the morning sunrise they all walked back to the Villa and little Caitlin thought to herself no matter how often one sees the sunrises and sunsets it is always like seeing it for the first time. It is truly beautiful. So many people miss it or take it for granted ... the grandeur of Earth and her creatures.

Soon they were ready to leave but before they did Caitlin spoke to Grandpapa, as he was about to get in his car. "Grandpapa ... I have added to the computer some access features so anyone who inspects the laptop will think they are accessing the data. What they will actually see though is nothing but an illusion. The real data on the stem cell research is further encrypted and hidden from inquiring eyes. That way if the authorities decide to search your computer and I believe they might they will not find anything of value to them. You are going to be fine. Remember that. And although this may sound strange since it has only been a few days but … I want to tell you I have grown to love you. We will meet again under different circumstances Grandpapa. I love you." Then she reached out her little arms for a hug and he bent down and she kissed him.

Grandpapa had tears in his eyes along with a great sadness and in a shaky voice he said, "I am so lucky to have met you … all of you. I will think of you always and wonder … and hope you are all okay."

Then the mother approached and kissed and hugged him and said, "Thank you so much for everything Lucas. You will always be in our hearts and I can't wait until we meet again … under different circumstances."

The father also hugged Lucas and thanked him as well. "My little girl has taught me so much about the importance of life and living. Staying here has been a blessing and I have found in you a new friend … a friend for life. Thank you Lucas and travel and live well."

And then the Grandpapa drove off with one final honk and a wave. The family all waved as they watched Grandpapa drive away. Then little Caitlin turned to Mommy and Daddy and said, "Time for us to leave Mommy and Daddy."

⌒⌒⌒

Just under three hours later Grandpapa was approaching the Switzerland - Italian border crossing. It was a beautiful morning and he took a deep breath as he approached the border crossing. The Swiss have the Schengen Agreement and usually there are no problems crossing the border. Once at the crossing his car was ordered to pull over. There was a security alert as he had been missing and was flagged as a person of interest that the Federal Intelligence Security wanted to question. Dr. Froehlich had been to Italy many times before and this was the first time he was ordered to pull over. He pulled over and two Frontier Guards came to speak to him at his car window. The local police showed up shortly after and asked him where he had been, what was his business in Italy, was anybody with him, where was he going now? Dr. Froehlich answered all questions as previously suggested by Caitlin. The guards had contacted the F.I.S. to determine what they should do with Dr. Froehlich? Did they want to detain him further? It seemed he did nothing wrong?

The call was forwarded to Ottinger of the F.I.S. The N.S.A. team were about to leave having no more information and at a dead end in the investigation when the call came in.

"Is it confirmed you have Dr. Froehlich?" Ottinger asked the Frontier Guard who identified himself as Thommen.

"Yes Sir … it is he but nothing seems amiss. What do you want to do?"

"Detain him. We'll be there within the hour as we want to question him." Ottinger ordered.

"Very well Sir." Thommen answered.

At that the guard passed the information to the police and had Dr. Froehlich exit his car for detainment.

"What is this all about?" The doctor demanded to know.

"We don't know Sir. Only that the F.I.S. wants to question you and they will be here within the hour.

"Well … I don't like this one bit. I want to get home. They better not be long." The doctor yelled as he was escorted away. The doctor sat waiting and time seemed to slow down.

Finally Ottinger showed up with three of his own officers and the N.S.A. team tagging alone. The group was very intimidating as they all approached Dr. Froehlich who was sitting in a chair.

"Let me do the speaking O'Reilly. He is a Swiss citizen." Ottinger stated. O'Reilly nodded but he didn't like it.

"Dr. Froehlich … I am Officer Ottinger of the Federal Intelligence Service. We have been looking for you since you left the train in Zurich a few days ago."

"What is this all about? What's the problem? I go away for a few days and when I return this is what happens? I don't understand what is going on? Is everything all right? Why am I being detained?"

"Well Sir. You were seen speaking to a family of three on the train that are of interest to us. Were you speaking to a family of three Americans on the train … a father and a mother of Chinese descent with a little girl?" Ottinger asked waiting for a reply and judging the doctor's response.

Dr. Froehlich played it perfectly. "Why yes … they did come and talk to me but I still don't understand what that has to do with anything?"

"We just have some questions for you. I am not at liberty to discuss why we want to talk with the family. Do you know where they went or where they were going after the train arrived in Zurich?" Ottinger continued.

"Well … they said they were on vacation but with no particular destination. We talked on the train and I found them to be very friendly. So we got talking and I suggested they come with me for a few days … to this Villa that I go to for retreats sometimes."

"And where is this Villa Dr. Froehlich?" Ottinger furrowed his brows.
"It is in very near Genoa."

"So they travelled with you in your car? Is that what you are saying Dr. Froehlich?" Ottinger probed further.

"Yes … we went directly from Zurich to the Villa. I didn't do anything wrong? The family seemed quite normal."

"What names did the family use?" Ottinger pressed further.

"The little girl said her name was Kirsten and the father said his name was Michael and the mother's name was … what was it again? It is kind of a strange name but it was Nuwa … yes … that is it." Dr. Froehlich seemed proud that he could remember that.

"What last name did they use?" Ottinger asked.

"Brennan." The doctor gave a short answer this time.

"Where exactly is the family now?" O'Reilly asked excitedly. Ottinger turned looking at O'Reilly and gave him a dirty look for budding in.

Dr. Froehlich looked at the stranger. He already knew they were Americans and their accents confirmed it. "I left the family at the Villa this morning but they left this morning when I left."

"Did they say where they were going?" Ottinger pressed for more information.

"Well … I did hear the parents talking in private … quite by accident that they were thinking of travelling to Barcelona?" The doctor answered looking at the rather large group.

"Did they talk about how they would be travelling perhaps?" Ottinger asked.

"No … just that they were thinking of going to Barcelona. Why in heavens name would you want to talk with that family?" The doctor asked in innocence.

Ottinger and O'Reilly looked at each other briefly … then O'Reilly said, "It is a matter of National Security. That is all I can tell you. Did the little girl seem … unusual?"

"Unusual? Unusual in what way?"

O'Reilly was starting to suspect … which was his nature. "I mean the little girl … did she seem smart to you or unusual in any way?" Then he added, "Was she carrying a … rag doll?"

"Why yes … she had a rag doll but she wasn't unusual. She seemed bright for a young child but nothing unusual. Just a normal family to me."

"Do you have any pictures of them Dr. Froehlich." Ottinger interjected.

"Ah … no I don't. Didn't think too?"

"Do you have any objections to us checking your phone Dr. Froehlich … and your computer?" Ottinger asked.

"Why no … of course not. I have nothing to hide." The doctor looked perplexed.

And so the phone was checked and the computer but everything seemed in order. There was nothing to suggest anything was amiss.

"One more question before we let you go Dr. Froehlich." Ottinger asked, "Do you know a Dr. Goldman?"

"Why yes … he is a good friend. Why do you ask about him?" The doctor seemed to squint his eyes.

"And when was the last time you called him or talked with him Dr. Froehlich?" Ottinger asked.

"Ah … I believe it was about ten days ago? Why?" The doctor asked suspiciously. "Is this all somehow connected to him?"

"So you know nothing about a phone call to Dr. Goldman during your train ride to Zurich? Nothing about a short call from a throw away phone then?" Ottinger and everyone looked suspiciously at the doctor.

"I know nothing about any such thing Sir." The doctor was starting to get pissed off. "Look … I have been fully cooperative but I would like to go now." The doctor looked directly at Ottinger.

"What are you plans when we release you Dr. Froehlich?"

"I am going directly home and then to work tomorrow."

"So you aren't leaving anywhere or have any other plans Sir." Ottinger looked directly at the doctor.

"No Sir. Now … am I free to go? I would like to go!" The doctor stated more loudly.

Dr. Froehlich was a man of influence and some wealth so Ottinger looked at O'Reilly and asked, "Do you have any further questions for him? I see no reason to detain him further."

"I have just one more question for him." O'Reilly replied. Then he turned and looked directly into Dr. Froehlich's eyes. "Do you have the address of this Villa that is near Genoa? And who owns the Villa?"

"Yes … I do have the address. If you give me a piece of paper and a pen I will write it down for you. It belongs to my friend Dr. Bohren. I will write his contact information if you want it!"

O'Reilly nodded his head yes but had a none-too-happy look on his face. Then Dr. Froehlich was released and he was in his vehicle and on his way again. His vehicle had been searched while he was detained but no contraband was found nor were any clues in the vehicle. Dr. Froehlich was glad to finally be on his way again although all he could think about was the family … and that little girl that called him "Grandpapa."

A few minutes later O'Reilly thanked Ottinger and then asked him, "I would appreciate if you would contact this Dr. Bohren to ask about the Villa. We will contact the Italian authorities so part of my team can search the Villa for any clues. The other half of my team is going to Barcelona to check that out."

The Swiss did follow up and talk with Dr. Bohren but the stories matched and so there was no new information. Ottinger informed O'Reilly and O'Reilly thanked him for the follow-up.

CHAPTER 15

DEAD ENDS: VANISHED

Ephesians 5:16
"Making the best use of the time, because the days are evil."

And so O'Reilly directed part of his N.S.A. team to the beautiful Villa on the Mediterranean that the family had stayed at with Dr. Froehlich but there was no one there. They met with Italian authorities but there were no traces that anyone was recently at the Villa. The Villa was private enough that not even one local knew the family had been there. And so the Villa turned out to be a dead end. Except for one thing. In the Villa on the Fazioli piano there was a single envelope. It had what seemed like Child's writing on the envelope. It was simply addressed to "Mrs. Baxter".

O'Reilly and agent Baxter and the rest of the N.S.A. team had rushed to Barcelona and met with the authorities there. Barcelona turned out to be a waste of time. There were no clues that the family had even come to Barcelona but they had to follow up what Dr. Froehlich had told them. O'Reilly and Baxter were contacted about the letter addressed to her.

"Open the letter and read it to us." Baxter commanded from Barcelona. O'Reilly listened as the phone was put on speaker.

"Okay … I'll open it now." The voice on the other side replied. All ears were listening in Barcelona and in the Villa all eyes were focused on the letter. They all wondered what was inside? Inside the letter was a single pink piece of letter size paper. On it were letters cut out and pasted like some ransom note you might see in a movie. The agent read it over the phone. "Here it is. It says … Mrs. Baxter … leave Mommy and Daddy and Me alone … or else! Then it is signed Caitlin."

O'Reilly responded first. "What the fucken hell is that bullshit? Is that all it says Chen? Anything else in the letter?"

"No Sir." Chen answered. "And the place is clean … real clean. No forensic evidence here that will be of use it seems. We checked and not a single or partial fingerprint anywhere … including the envelope. No DNA remnants either."

Baxter hadn't responded to the letter. She was too much in shock but she had a bad feeling about this. She didn't usually have such strong intuition but her feelings about this were that it might end up badly. She couldn't explain it but it was there in her gut.

O'Reilly seemed to yell into the phone, "We're coming to see for ourselves! We'll be there shortly and we will be landing at the Genoa Cristoforo Colombo Aeroporto. Safeguard that letter until we get there. We'll be there within a couple of hours and meet you at the Villa. Keep looking ... maybe there is something else."

"Yes Sir," Agent Chen replied. "We'll standby and keep looking." And at that the call ended.

Everywhere that N.S.A. searched and having released an International Wanted List to all surrounding Countries there was nothing. The footprints had vanished and there was nothing to do but return to the United States. The N.S.A. team was pissed but none more so than O'Reilly. On the flight back the team talked about it. What had happened? How did the family ... that should be easy to track ... just disappear from the face of the Earth?

O'Reilly spoke to his team on the Military jet as it headed home. "I tell you this! There is no way that family is working alone! No way in Hell! They've had help! They've got connections and the more we know about this is that this is big! We are very concerned that our security at the N.S.A. has been compromised ... and compromised in the worst way. We didn't even know about it at first. We are going full out and we will find them!" O'Reilly looked at his team almost in disgust it seemed ... his nostrils flared and his eyes red with anger. He definitely needed to take some anger management courses.

Baxter spoke as second in command. "I agree … in fact we all agree with you Sir. We have checked with our allies for every possible avenue of escape. Every airport, train, vehicle, boats and what I have trouble explaining is how they did it? I mean it is a family of three and the family has a white husband, a Chinese mother, and little girl of mixed descent. They should be easy to spot. The disturbing fact is that they or some group are somehow controlling the cameras en route and also from what we know our satellites are not being permitted to take pictures of them. It seems that sometimes our satellites are shutdown as a decoy and that the family wasn't in the area. That is high tech stuff … very high tech and especially worrisome. We are having difficulty breaking the encryptions on the computer we seized in the house back in San Jose, the bank accounts and finance accounts all closed by the family under their two fake names … Brennan and Gray. They had to have this all planned ahead of time. We need to find them and find them fast. The trail is cold now and perhaps Sir we need an incentive?"

O'Reilly nodded his head. He liked what he heard but he was still mighty pissed off. Sometimes it took a long time for him to cool down. He already had a few reprimands and write-ups for his … temper tantrums. He was scheduled to go for some counseling but so far he had evaded that.

"I agree Baxter but our allies suck! The Germans … the French … the Swiss … they all bloody fucken suck." Suddenly O'Reilly caught himself. Swearing wasn't the problem but him speaking about so-called friends of the United States was. He realized what he was saying. "Okay … anything I say here about this is off the record!" He eyed each member of his team. One guy … Sandford had a bit of a smirk. "Wipe that bloody fucken smile off your face Sandford! I'm not pussyfooting around here. The allies do suck! Those Swiss should have been able to do more … much more. Same for those bloody Krauts. And the French are only slightly better. But no one … and I mean no one talks or mentions anything about what I said here about the allies. We don't want a political or diplomatic scandal disrupting our mission." O'Reilly sent dagger eyes to his team … especially Sandford, who now wasn't smiling at all.

After a few seconds of awkward silence Baxter spoke. "Sir ... the suspects weren't even in Germany and in fairness the Swiss and French had no chance as the suspects were long gone it seems."

O'Reilly gave Baxter a dirty look but she was right.

Baxter continued, "Sir ... the incentive idea? We need a motivation for others to find these people and considering the importance I would suggest that a reward should be considered a high priority. And Sir, ... we need them alive for intelligence gathering."

O'Reilly turned to Baxter ... his heart still beating like he was climbing some great hill. He took a deep breath trying to slow his heart and then replied, "Yes Baxter ... very good. I will mention to my superiors about a reward first thing. In the meantime I want the team to talk among themselves and perhaps we can figure something out." Then O'Reilly walked to a different part of the jet for a bit of privacy and made the call.

〜〈〉〜

Nothing happened for the next couple of weeks. The United States Intelligence Community, or the I.C. that has seventeen separate governmental agencies worked together to collect information and find the family. Agents in the field were on the alert and using their intelligence contacts to track down and find the suspects. And then thirteen days later the first break in the case came. And it was the French Authorities and the D.G.S.I. that did it. They had been checking the visitors to the Eiffel Tower around the times the family was alleged to have visited the tourist attraction. They had found an old couple, a Mr. and Mrs. Kubera that had talked to the alleged suspects at the top of the tower. There wasn't any real information about the family from the conversation except the fact that the little girl seemed very smart and had a lot of knowledge about the Eiffel Tower ... and the Air Pollution Index (API) of the area. What was important was that the old couple had been taking a few pictures while on vacation. And in one of those pictures the family was in the background. This might be the first real picture of the suspects. It was only one picture but it was something at least. The French Authorities made a copy of the picture and sent it quickly to the N.S.A. team. Agent Baxter and Agent White were called into a room when the picture arrived at the National Security Agency. There was a bit of an excitement in the air. This could be their first break if it was true … if it was the family. Sure they had composite sketches of the suspects but a real photograph … well … that would be much better.

Agent Baxter and White looked at the picture. "That's the family!" Baxter quickly confirmed. She was excited.

"Yes … that's definitely the family. No doubt about it Sir." Agent White added.

"All right!" O'Reilly semi squealed out. It wasn't much but now they had the faces of the suspects. "We'll send it out to all our contacts immediately. We'll get them!" O'Reilly almost said we'll get those bastards but his superior was there and he caught himself just in the nick of time. His superior had already told him to tone the language down and act more professional a few weeks earlier.

Weatherly was in the room but seemed less impressed with the find. He realized they still had to find and capture the family but this was a good start. "Good work team. We will send it out and I'll be sure to thank the French Authorities for their help. We still have to find them but now … we have a clear picture. I will also let you know that we have decided on a reward for capture. We are confirming and letting our allies know there is a ten million dollar reward for a live capture."

Baxter looked at Weatherly. She wasn't happy with what she considered a low dollar amount. Especially considering the risk factors. Still … it was early and maybe that ten million dollars would get the allies more interested and focused on finding the suspects.

~~~

And then in the next few days all hell broke loose. The New York Authorities had finally traced the source of the phone call they received about the flight 1536 plane crash that killed everyone on board months earlier. It wasn't easy but finally they traced the call from a Mr. Michael and Nuwa Brennan residence in San Jose. News media and authorities flooded the house and the N.S.A. became aware of it. A little girl had called the airport just a few hours before the jet crashed warning them the jet would crash. They had given the jet a quick check but found nothing wrong and the jet took off on its doomed flight. When the N.S.A., the F.B.I., and the C.I.A. heard about the phone call by their suspects warning of a jet crashing, meetings were quickly held and people were interviewed. They had a recording of the phone call and it was the little girl calling it in. The media got wind of it and when it went mainstream on all the major networks that is when all hell broke loose. Were the family terrorists? It doesn't take much for a fear mongering feeding frenzy to build. It must be a terrorist attack but terrorists don't phone in giving a warning first?

~~~

In an apartment just off from San Jose sat a woman who just happened to be watching the television. It was the homeless lady that little Caitlin and her mother had met just a few months earlier in that grocery store parking lot. Sarah Starr was her name and that act of kindness resulted in Sarah getting a job and an apartment and putting her life back together. The news of the little girl phoning in about a jet crashing just hours before it crashed was on every channel. There were also reports about sightings of the wanted American family that had been seen in other parts of the World. The little girl and the mother on the news were the same people that stopped to talk with Sarah in that parking lot. Sarah would never forget the mother and daughter's act of kindness ... and especially the miracle that happened. They were the ones that not only gave her groceries and money but Sarah was positive that little girl cured her of her brain tumor somehow. Sarah had heard about the jet crashing months earlier in New York and about a little girl phoning in but thought nothing of it. Sarah was certain the mother and little girl weren't terrorists. She was positive of that but that little girl had somehow made her tumor go away? The doctors were all amazed her cancerous tumor had disappeared and so quickly? Totally gone and they had no explanation? They themselves called it a miracle. Sarah felt something when the little girl touched her and then the little girl had whispered that she would be all right … it's gone! So Sarah called the media to report her contact and experience with the mother and the little girl. Sarah meant well and wanted to help the family. The news media was wrong. They weren't terrorists. The networks ate it up. They followed up and checked with the doctors and they had no explanation how Sarah's medical condition changed? How she was cured? When it aired on the news it just added fuel to the fire to find that little girl. She was obviously very special. And the media had a picture of the family that went on the networks. The United States upped the reward for the little girl and family but especially for little Caitlin.

There were occasional sightings of the family over the course of the next eighteen months in several parts of the World. Sightings were reported in Canada in Montreal and then Victoria. There were also sightings in United States in Nashville and Pittsburg. Reports came in from Stockholm and then Buenos Aires that the family was there. All the reports were checked out but they turned out false.

There first actual confirmed sightings happened after the Italian trail went dead and the family was spotted in Sydney Harbour, Australia, and so agents were sent there and although people remembered seeing the family and especially the little girl they were no longer there. And then there was a sighting in Bandar Seri Begawan, Brunei and so agents followed them there. Same result. It seemed no matter where the sightings the family had vanished before they arrived. The third confirmed sighting was in Angkor, Cambodia, the fourth in Ulan Bator, Mongolia, the fifth in Almaty, Kazakhstan, the sixth in Thimphu, Bhutan but all had the same results. No footprints in the sand could be found except that yes …the family had been there but were now gone. It was reported that the family had changed appearances slightly … or tried to change appearances by changing hair color, make-up, and the three always wore dark sunglasses and hats.

The family had been to all those places but had only stayed as long as they could. The parents were tired of all the travelling and hiding. It was exciting and many times breathtaking to visit those wondrous places but it was taking its toll on them. Little Caitlin could see that and so she made a decision. Caitlin would find a place to settle for longer this time … a place where they could rest and be more human again. So for the next nine months there were no sightings of the family.

The family had travelled to the city known as the "City of Eternal Spring." It was Kunming, China that the family settled in. The language spoken in Kunming is Mandarin and both the Mommy and the little girl were fluent. Actually the little girl was fluent in every language. The father spoke some Mandarin but he wasn't quite fluent. His wife and daughter had been teaching him the language. The family rented an apartment. It was a beautiful place, the capital of Yunnan and when the season is in full-bloom the flowers and trees are spectacular. Reds, blues, yellows and greens were popping up everywhere in the highly manicured parks, lane dividers, boulevards and any other small patches of land. Of all these flowers some of the most spectacular are the cherry blossoms known as yinghua and the flowering crabapple known as haitanghua. The blossoms of these two trees are as stunning as they are short-lived.

The family loved it there. They managed to see many spectacular sights in the area and enjoyed conversing with the people who welcomed them. The family visited sites such as the Yunnan Nationalities Village, the Yunnan Nationalities Museum, Green Lake, Dongchuan Red Land, the Kunming Golden Temple, Yunnan University … to name only a few.

It was a paradise to them and they managed to forget for a short time that the most powerful Country in the World was hunting for them. There were many looking for them and they took no days off. It's all they did … every day … was to search the earth … the eyes of the satellites in the sky looking down … their agents in the field asking questions … offering money for information … searching. It was only a matter of time.

CHAPTER 16

DISCOVERED: ACROSS THE WORLD

1 Corinthians 13:13
"So now faith, hope, and love abide, these three; but the greatest of these is love."

It had been two and a half years since the beginnings of the hunt. United States was relentless. They had developed a Code Name for the hunt for the little girl. It was simply "Y.S.B." or the hunt for a Young Supreme Being. It was the greatest, most expensive, and in reality the most important hunt for a human in the history of mankind … but it was all for the wrong reasons.

And so the United States government increased the reward … by a lot. Other Countries were becoming aware something was important here. Those other Country's own intelligence reports confirmed there was something about this little girl that the United States wanted badly. And so other Countries starting offering rewards and sent agents out to track and find the little girl and her parents. The United States argued that the suspects were first and foremost citizens of the United States and that if captured they must be returned to the United States or there would be dire consequences. However the other Countries weren't buying that argument. They wanted the little girl for their own evil purposes. And so each Country offered rewards for the little girl's safe capture. A full out hunt was on and the World was suddenly becoming even smaller for the family.

⌒⟨⎮⟩⌒

The National Security Agency in Maryland held a meeting and Weatherly, O'Reilly and Baxter were there. Baxter and O'Reilly had been transferred there some six months earlier but Agent Baxter also worked in other various offices when needed. She was on her way up in the system. There were many other top personnel at the meeting to discuss all options for a successful capture and to speed up the capture.

A Senior I.T. agent spoke first about the computer that they seized two and a half years ago. "As you know regarding the computer seized at the residence in San Jose … we are no closer now then we were at the start to accessing the data inside. And it looks like we may never get into the computer? We have had our top people in the field trying to get in and solve this computer but it is not like anything we have ever seen before? We are still working on finding a way in but the security system is constantly changing. We now believe the only way to view its contents would be for the owners ... the family to access the system."

"Consider this. That computer would not require that such extreme measures to get in would be needed unless there was something extremely important inside. We would be well advised to think about that. It is when thinking about that and that it is not what we know ... but what we don't know that is extremely worrisome." Weatherly stated to the group.

O'Reilly then added, "And the short clip we have of the little girl and the mathematic formulas ... why we can find no math expert in the world that can understand it? They all agree though that it is real ... it is not mumbo jumbo ... and that the math has meanings we only partially understand. Even after all this time we still are not sure but the experts think it may be some formulation for a new energy that theoretically could be used for space travel but we aren't certain? They all agree it is some pretty advanced stuff." That set the group off with more discussions on the importance of finding these suspects.

Baxter then started the group on another discussion. "And the fact that we have proof that the little girl called the airport in New York to warn about that jet crash just hours before it crashed. The findings of the crash was that it was not a terrorist attack and that it was exactly as the little girl reported ... a mechanical failure of the right engine. That leads to a conclusion that the girl may have some kind of psychic abilities as well. I believe it is no coincidence that all these things have happened ... the hacking of our defense systems, our satellites being compromised and controlled or the loss of our satellite's ability to track or take pictures for a short time, that coincides with the areas the family were in at the time, the cameras going down where the family was, the power going down in the hotel in Paris without any explanations, the security of that computer, the advanced mathematic formulas, and the fact that the family has been able to evade capture for so long. We have no proof that they have accomplices or conspirators to help them but that there is only the three of them and not some larger group. At least as far as we know."

They were all nodding their heads as all these facts were being recounted. More discussions followed. It was a frustrated group. And if that wasn't enough Agent Baxter added the "Coup de grace." "We have also been tracking Dr. Lucas Froehlich … the doctor who was on the train with the family from Paris to Zurich, and then the doctor went to the Villa in Italy for a few days with the family." All eyes were on Baxter. "It seems the doctor has suddenly been making some very advanced findings in some stem cell research areas … all since meeting with the family … the little girl. In fact it is suffice to say that perhaps this new knowledge isn't all his doing. That he had help … from Caitlin perhaps?"

"Just exactly what are you saying Baxter?" Weatherly prodded. "That the little girl is some sort of stem cell expert too?"

"Well Sir … we are now certain we are dealing with a super advanced intelligence in the girl. It isn't the parents. The evidence doesn't support it. We all know there is a grave National threat here. We can agree to that but even more grave and concerning is that we don't fully know exactly what we are dealing with?" Baxter answered. "And other Countries have for a few months now been monitoring this with great interest. That little girl is of importance to many Countries and they are … excuse me for saying this Sir but it is true … all are not friends of the United States. We have to think … and prepare for the possibility that some other Country may capture the girl … and reap the benefits of that super intelligence."

No one mentioned the letter left in the Villa for Agent Baxter because well … they all thought it was just some little girl warning to leave her and her family alone. Baxter still felt uneasy about that letter though. She never expressed it to her superiors … or anyone else.

Weatherly sat back in his chair and there was a scary silence in the room for the next several seconds or so. Weatherly cleared his throat. "Are we all in agreement here?" Weatherly looked around the room and the entire twenty-two were all nodding their heads in agreement. "Anyone disagree with this?" Weatherly looked but there was not a one. "I have to agree with Agent Baxter. There is far too much at risk. What is the reward at now? I believe it is twenty-five million dollars ... yes ... it is at twenty-five million dollars. That is the same as Osama Bin Laden's reward. I will meet with the President and Council about raising the reward money."

"Sir?" Baxter interjected.

"Yes Agent Baxter ... what is it?" Weatherly and the group looked over at Baxter.

"Well Sir ... two things. First ... when we were hunting for Osama Bin Laden other Countries weren't so interested in finding him so much ... at least not to the level we were. It would only be for the money and so twenty-five million would be low for a Country but good for an individual. Now since other Countries have a real interest in the girl and considering the risks involved if they get her first ... I would really suggest a very high reward. Perhaps one hundred million dollars." At that comment there was some uneasiness in the room. "That would be much more of a motivation for finding her. Secondly ... the last time we offered the twenty-five million for Osama Bin Laden the reward wasn't paid out since we considered it our service men that got him. I might suggest that this time we offer the reward to be paid to any individual non-exclusive of who they are. I say this realizing we have exceptional service men and women in the field but really Sir the importance of this capture and the need for expediency, we should be sure we don't take any shortcuts.

What followed was an hour-long discussion about options. Weatherly told the group before ending the meeting, "I will ask to meet with the President and the Council as soon as possible."

Weatherly and the top N.S.A. officials met with the President within a few hours and the reward for $100 million dollars was approved. And it got immediate responses when word went out. The hunt intensified. All the Countries in the World wondered further what was so important to find this little girl although whispers had already circulated around the globe. That there walked on the planet a super intelligence in the form of a little girl who was not yet seven years old. And that she may be able to see future events … and cure brain tumors … and much more.

⌒⁊⟨⋏⟩⌒

Little Caitlin sensed it just days before it happened. She sensed they were discovered. So she broke the bad news to her parents. They would be leaving China and with so many looking for them they decided the safest way to travel was to split up. Daddy would leave first and then a few hours later Mommy and Caitlin would leave on a jet. The Chinese authorities had begun looking for them. They heard the wanted family might be in Kunming and so that is where the Chinese agents went to look first.

The father under disguise left China first and hours later landed in Rio de Janeiro. He didn't like leaving his family but he had total confidence in his little girl and she said it was the only way … the safest way for them to travel now. Searching for the three of them as a group would be just too easy to spot. He landed in Rio and waited for his wife and daughter. A few hours later the mother and daughter boarded the big jet bound for Rio and they too were in disguise. There was a relief in the mother when the jet left the Kunming Changshui International Airport and would be landing at the Rio de Janeiro/Galeão–Antonio Carlos Jobim International Airport.

"Don't worry Mommy. We will be with Daddy soon."

They talked with no strangers this time and the little girl read books appropriate for her age. She was bored to death but at least that wouldn't make anyone suspicious. That they couldn't possibly be a part of the family everyone was looking for. When the jet landed in Rio they got their little bit of luggage, hired a taxi and travelled to the meeting spot where Daddy would be. The Pousada Chez Moi - Chez Toi Hotel in Cabo Frio, which was a little less than a two-hour drive up the coast. The family was aware that Brazil had an extradition treaty with the United States but they were not staying long and thought they could get lost for the expected two day stay. Daddy had been told to go to Cabo Frio and wait for them. Not to meet them at the airport since the three of them stood out now like a zit on a teenager's face the night of the prom … especially the three of them at the airport. Even in Rio the public and authorities were aware of an American family that was wanted with an incredible reward of one hundred million dollars … and it was tax-free.

The drive seemed long though in reality it wasn't that long. Compounded with the very long flight from Kunming it was a long journey. Mommy and Caitlin did sleep in the big jet but still they both felt tired and would be happy to rest … even if they were only going to stay for two days. The taxi arrived in Cabo Frio and dropped them off. The whole area seemed a thing of beauty.

"Hello … I'm Mrs. Black and this is my daughter Brittany. I believe my husband arrived here a few hours earlier and registered us." The Mommy was talking to the girl at the reception desk.

"Ah … yes Mrs. Black. He mentioned your expected arrival. Here is the key to your room and if we may be of further service please do not hesitate to ask us. We want your stay to be as lovely as possible. The room is on the first floor just down the hallway to the left."

It was when they first inquired at the reception desk of the Hotel that little Caitlin sensed something was wrong. Caitlin's face showed her sudden concern. The little girl looked at her Mommy and showed concern … and anger. The Mommy wasn't looking at Caitlin though. Caitlin was almost seven years old and each day her intelligence and gifts had continued to develop. Caitlin now had the ability to sense … or trace certain brain patterns in people … like a signature or a fingerprint. She had the ability to focus in on a person she knew or had met and could find them anywhere in the World just by concentrating on them. It was in a very real sense like the electronic chip someone might put in their pet dog or cat … but much more sophisticated … and much more powerful. But she couldn't really find Daddy's signature. Caitlin knew he wasn't dead and she also knew that even if he were hidden in some room or vault her senses would be able to detect him. Even if he was surrounded by lead or no matter what the material. Caitlin came to the conclusion there could be only one explanation. Daddy had been drugged enough to effect his brain wave patterns. Caitlin concentrated harder on finding Daddy and then she did locate him. He had been put on a jet that had left hours earlier and had been abducted back to the United States.

It was when they were in the room and Mommy called out to Daddy and got no answer that Caitlin told her Mommy what happened.

"Daddy's not here Mommy?" Little Caitlin said angrily. "They got him!"

"What do you mean they got him? What do you mean? Who got him? Where is he Caitlin? Mommy was now screaming but mostly crying. "Oh my dear GOD!" she sobbed as she collapsed on a chair in the room … her hands covering her face.

Caitlin ran to her Mommy and hugged her and cried right along with her. Then a minute later … Mommy still bawling … Caitlin said, "Come to the window with me Mommy." Caitlin looked outside and was holding onto her Mommy's hand. "They took Daddy out there." She pointed out towards the beach area. "They drugged him and put him on a jet to take him back to the United States. There are still a few agents here looking for us now but we won't have to worry about them Mommy. I know we just got here but we are leaving right now. You and I are going to the United States." Caitlin said still looking out the window. The little girl was angry … very angry and her anger was growing. She was angrier than Mommy had ever seen her before ... and that scared Mommy. Not for herself but for anyone that got in this little girl's way. Now she was hunting for Daddy! And she wouldn't stop until she found him.

But first there was a phone call to make to the N.S.A. Headquarters in Fort George E. Mead in Maryland. Caitlin picked up the phone and didn't even dial. The phone did it all itself just by Caitlin's thoughts. On the third ring someone answered the phone.

"Agent Baxter." The receiver of the call answered.

"Agent Baxter! I warned you! Let my Daddy go! Let him go now! He hasn't done anything wrong." A little girl's voice responded angrily.

"Caitlin? Caitlin? Is that you Caitlin?" Agent Baxter frantically asked although she knew it was the little girl. Baxter was waving her arms and fingers to the other agents in the room ... letting them know to trace this call. She put the call on loudspeaker so everyone could hear ... including her boss O'Reilly. "We need to talk with you Caitlin. We'll let your Daddy go after you talk with us in person. We are your friends Caitlin and we just want to clear some things up. After we talk we will let you all go. I promise."

There was a slight pause and then Caitlin spoke. "Your breathing is faster ... your heart rate is up ... your pupils are dilated ... your nostrils are flared ... your G.S.R. levels are elevated ... and your brain wave patterns have changed. I can sense that. You are lying! You are not my friend! I'm coming to get my Daddy! I know he's there! I warned you! There's nothing you can do to stop me! No one can help you now! You'll all be sorry!" She yelled into the phone and then she abruptly hung up.

CHAPTER 17

WRATH: THE HUNTER BECOMES THE HUNTED

Isaiah 5:29

"Its roaring is like a lioness, and it roars like young lions; it growls as it seizes the prey and carries it off with no one to deliver it."

Caitlin directed Mommy to phone and make reservations to fly from Rio de Janeiro to the Baltimore - Washington International Thurgood Marshall Airport. The flight would leave in five hours. Then a call was made for a taxi to take them from Cabo Frio to the Rio de Janeiro Airport. The clerk at the desk was surprised at the fast checkout.

"But you just got here? Is anything wrong with the accommodations?" The clerk asked.

"No ... but we just received some bad news and we must go to the United States as soon as possible." The mother answered. Her eyes were red from all the crying.

"I'm so sorry to hear that." The clerk didn't quite know what to say.

Mommy and Caitlin waited outside the hotel for the taxi. The taxi was pulling up when suddenly five N.S.A. agents were running towards them in the distance. Caitlin had already sensed their presence and turned to see them running towards her. They had their guns out. Mommy didn't see them or what suddenly happened to them. They all just suddenly dropped to the ground. Mommy and Caitlin got in the taxi and left for the drive back to Rio de Janeiro. Soon they were on board the big jet heading towards the Baltimore - Washington International Thurgood Marshall Airport. It was another long flight and Caitlin was thinking about her Daddy. She was going to get Daddy and there was no one on the planet that could stop her.

⌒⌒⌒

At the National Security Agency a call came in that was forwarded to O'Reilly. The call came in under the code name "Y.S.B."

"O'Reilly here." He almost shouted into the phone. Baxter was with him and he put the phone on speaker.

"Sir ... this is Walken!" The agent yelled back very distressed.

"Walken ... do you have the package? Do you have good" ... But O'Reilly never got to finish.

"No Sir! They have escaped!" Walken screamed into the phone.

"What do you mean they escaped Walken?" O'Reilly yelled back.

"Sir ... you really need to listen to me! Do not interrupt until I stop!" Walken raised his voice even louder. "Sir ... we had them dead to rights! We had them at the front of the Hotel in Cabo Frio and we were running to them as they were getting into the taxi! Oh my GOD Sir ... Oh my GOD! You are not going to believe this! The little girl definitely saw us when suddenly we were all forced to the ground! We couldn't move ... none of us ... when I tried to stand up!" Walken started crying while on the phone. "Sir ... when I tried to stand up ... holy shit ... my legs ... they're gone! They're just gone? I don't have no legs Sir! How can that be?" Then the agent started crying like a baby.

"What the fuck Walken?" What do you mean your legs are gone? Were you hit?" O'Reilly yelled back. "Is that what you mean?"

Walken stopped crying for a second. It was obvious he was in shock. "Sir ... no ... no one fired at us! Our legs Sir ... all of us ... all our legs ... they're just ... gone ... at the hips? No blood ... no nothin ... not even physical pain! It is like we never had legs? We are all at the Hospital Municipal da Mulher in Cabo Frio! The doctor is looking at us! He thinks we were born without legs! He doesn't believe us!"

"What do ya mean your legs are all gone? That doesn't make sense?" O'Reilly was trying to understand the impossible.

"Sir … the little girl did it! Jesus Christ Sir … we got no more legs?" Walken tried not to cry as he spoke. "What the hell is going on Sir? What aren't you telling us about that little girl?" Walken screamed back at O'Reilly.

"Who's there with you Walken?" O'Reilly commanded. He didn't believe it. He thought Walken was having a mental breakdown or something.

"Sir … we're all here in the same room at the hospital! All five of us! The doctor has left us for now!" Walken blubbered.

""Put me on speaker Walken." O'Reilly commanded.

"Okay Sir … you're on speaker now." Walken sniffled back.

O'Reilly heard a bunch of men … his men … crying like little babies. "Wilson, Bender, Stall, Germaine … can you all hear me?"

All O'Reilly could hear was a bunch of people sobbing in the background … and afraid. Then he heard someone trying to speak. "Sir … this is Bender! Please Sir … please Sir … please … if you see the little girl … please tell her to give me my legs back!" And then the phone went dead … although no one hung up.

O'Reilly and Baxter stood in the room looking at each other with mouths open. O'Reilly said it first. "What the HELL is going on here? Those agents are obviously suffering from some kind of delusion … or mind control?"

"Sir … I got a feeling about this and it isn't good! I can't explain it but we better get ready. The girl's coming and she said we better not hurt her father. You heard the call … that we'd all be sorry." Baxter looked in some shock herself.

O'Reilly fired back, "This is such bullshit! She's just a little girl for GOD's sake! Check the flights from Rio. She's probably on it." After checking with the airlines it was confirmed. The mother and daughter were on the flight and would be landing at the Baltimore - Washington International Thurgood Marshall Airport in seven hours. "Good!" O'Reilly shot back. "We'll be ready for them! We'll be waiting for them! We got em now! We'll settle this bullshit once and for all!"

On the big jet in the middle of the night the Mommy sat beside her little girl worried what was going to happen. Even she had no idea what her little girl was capable of.

"Caitlin darling … what are you going to do when we land? Remember your promise not to hurt anyone? Maybe we can clear all this up now?" The Mommy didn't really believe that though.

Caitlin who had been staring straight ahead the whole time turned her little head and answered, "I'm going to get Daddy back and I am going to end this once and for all! I remember the promise that I would try not hurt anyone Mommy but they are hurting Daddy … trying to get information from him about me … about us. For that there is no mercy! Judge not, that you be not judged. For with the judgment you pronounce you will be judged, and with the measure you use it will be measured to you." Then little Caitlin took hold of Mommy's hand and looked lovingly at her. "Try not to worry but today you will see things that will frighten you but do not be afraid … for I am with you."

The Mommy stared at the Child of her Womb and wondered … wondered about today … and wondered what was going to happen? She was worried for her husband and her daughter but even more she was worried about the people in her daughter's way.

"Oh God Caitlin." She sighed as the big jet flew into the dark night towards an Armageddon.

CHAPTER 18

OMNIPOTENT POWER UNLEASHED

Genesis 6:5

"And GOD saw that the wickedness of man was great in the earth, and that every imagination of the thoughts of his heart was only evil continually."

There was chaos at the Baltimore - Washington International Thurgood Marshall Airport as they prepared for the arrival. The N.S.A., the F.B.I., the C.I.A., the Police and Airport Authorities were all on the highest alert. They didn't quite know what to expect … except there was an order to hold fire and to not shoot the little girl. They knew there was some sort of an "altercation" in South America and that some agents may have been hurt but it was not reported how they were hurt or to what extent? O'Reilly had trouble believing what his agents in Cabo Frio told him and decided it was too far fetched to tell them … the team the details. O'Reilly had sent other N.S.A. agents to the airport to apprehend the mother and the little girl when the jet landed. He and Baxter stayed back at the N.S.A. Headquarters waiting for word of the capture and were preparing for interrogation. The father was there … in a room … tired from hours upon hours of interrogation. He didn't tell them anything really though. Not that he saw his daughter doing miracles even he couldn't believe. In the two and a half years on the run he had seen his daughter continue to evolve … as her intelligence and powers continued to increase even more. He waited … knowing that his daughter was coming … coming to rescue him and make all his suffering go away.

A few hours later the big jet was making the final approach to the airport runway and the landing gear came down. Caitlin looked at her Mommy sitting beside her and Mommy was looking out the window. Trying to look ahead to the airport to catch a glimpse if anything seemed out of place … to try to determine if they were waiting for them. She was nervous and Caitlin sensed it.

"Mommy … do you know what day it is today?"

Mommy looked at her daughter wondering what she meant? The she realized it and suddenly gave a half smile and said, "Yes I do honey. It is your birthday and you are seven years old today." She gave her daughter a kiss and said, "Happy Birthday Caitlin. Some birthday huh?"

"I love you Mommy. And I love Daddy too! And we are going to have a birthday party tonight …the three of us. You … Daddy and Me." The little girl whispered, "But I need you to know some things. They are waiting for us. Don't be afraid though. I will take care of everything. Always stay beside me no matter what. I will be holding your hand when we exit the jet. We won't be getting our luggage."

"Okay but I feel like I am going to be sick to my stomach." The Mommy answered. She felt understandably queasy.

"You'll be okay Mommy … I promise." Then she stared at the door where they would be exiting the jet. She grabbed her Mommy's hand and waited for the big jet to land.

As the jet finally touched down on the tarmac they could see all the police vehicles with their lights flashing waiting for them. Many of the passengers saw it too and they were nervous and anxious in the jet as they wondered what was going on? Was there some kind of mechanical problem they didn't know about? Were there terrorists on board? It looked a bit like World War Three out there. The pilots had been notified hours earlier that there were fugitives on board but that no action was to be taken. The on board Air Marshall was to do nothing. They were explicit about that. The jet taxied through the runways and then off to the main building where passengers would exit. The passengers would exit the jet and then walk a short distance to the arrival entrance.

Then the pilot spoke over the intercom to the passengers. "We are asking all passengers to remain seated for the moment. Please be patient and we will let you know when you can exit the jet shortly? We are sorry for the inconvenience."

Many passengers started asking the flight attendants what was happening? Why all the police and emergency vehicles outside? But the attendants were not informed either. They knew nothing.

Caitlin turned to her Mommy and said, "Time to get up and leave Mommy. Just follow me."

Mommy looked at her daughter in sheer shock and said, "Leave? … Now? … Are you sure Caitlin?" Her face extremely flushed.

"Let's go now Mommy!" Caitlin was holding her Mommy's hand as they both got up from their seats and were walking towards the exit door that was still locked. In her other hand she was carrying Sally … her rag doll.

Two flight attendants approached the pair and one of them said, "I'm sorry but you will have to go back to your seats ma'am. No one can leave the aircraft right now."

Little Caitlin stood before the attendants, "All that outside … all that commotion is for us." And then the exit door to the jet opened all by itself. But really it was the little girl's mind opening it. "Stand aside." The little girl ordered.

The passengers that could hear and see were in shock … as well as the two flight attendants but they did stand aside.

Mommy and Caitlin went to the door and looked out to the tarmac below and the many officers and vehicles that were there. There must have been two hundred officers and over eighty vehicles … all for them … to capture her.

"Walk with me Mommy and hold onto the railing. Watch your step." Caitlin surveyed the scene that looked surreal. Her little face could not hide her anger. They walked to the bottom of the stairs and then they were standing on the tarmac as hundreds of guns and scopes were upon them.

"Put your hands up and stay right there and don't move!" Came a single voice over the loud speaker.

Mommy raised her one hand over her head while her other hand still grasped little Caitlin's hand. "Mommy ... put your hand down! You don't need to raise it." Little Caitlin looked up at her Mommy.

The passengers in the jet were jammed up all looking out the windows to see what was happening outside? They wanted a better look. Then twenty law enforcement officers rushed towards the pair with their guns drawn with everyone shouting at the mother and little Caitlin. And then just as suddenly all the officers stopped. Nothing was moving and all was silent. Even the slight breeze had stopped. Mommy noticed it right away when it happened. She turned to look at her little girl who was smiling and then she noticed over her daughter's shoulder there was a very big jet about to land on a distant runway. But the jet was just still in the sky ... it wasn't moving either. Caitlin had stopped time.

Caitlin pulled on her Mommy's hand and said, "Follow me Mommy ... our ride is here."

Mommy being pulled by Caitlin was looking all around. Everything in sight was ... frozen in time. Even the many people in the main building peering out the windows were not moving. They went to one of the SUV vehicles and there was a driver inside. He too was frozen. They pulled the frozen driver out of the vehicle. They closed the front driver's door and opened the back doors ... then both slid into the back seat and closed the door. Then Caitlin said, "Be sure to buckle up Mommy."

"My God Caitlin! They're all like this? How far did you stop time?" Mommy asked.

"Just the local area. I will start time again when we are on our way ... away from all this."

And then the car started driving … with no driver. Mommy started screaming but little Caitlin said, "Don't worry Mommy … I know the way and how to drive."

Mommy just stared at her daughter. "But we're in the backseat and no one … is at the wheel?"

Little Caitlin looked at her Mommy like what is the big deal? "It's okay Mommy … I'm a good driver … we won't crash. It isn't far so try to enjoy the ride. Think of it like an invisible chauffeur." Caitlin smiled at her nervous Mommy.

"An invisible chauffeur?" Mommy noticed Caitlin wasn't even looking where the SUV was going but she had her head down staring at Sally. "But you aren't even looking where we're going?"

"It's okay Mommy. I can see. I see everything now."

Mommy just shook her head as she stared past the empty front seat and the windshield as the SUV sped off.

Caitlin wasn't interested in the U.S. Cyber Command or the Central Security Service Buildings nearby. As they were approaching the N.S.A. Headquarters there were a few checkpoints they had to pass. The vehicle's windows were heavily tinted and so not much could be seen from outside looking in. The vehicle slowed down and stopped at the first checkpoint. The driver's window rolled down and the guards peered in and then realized there was no driver. They saw the Mommy and the little girl in the back seat. "We're going in to get Daddy!" The little girl shouted.

"What the hell?" The guards looked confused and perplexed. The guards quickly drew their guns but they too were suddenly frozen. The gate rose … Caitlin made the driver's window go up and then the SUV was driving again.

They went to another checkpoint but this time Caitlin just pre-froze the guards and then she swung the gate open with her mind.

The SUV parked at the front entrance and the two exited and started heading up the stairs to the main building. Then Caitlin unfroze everyone, the airport scene, and the guards at the N.S.A. entrance points. At the airport all hell was breaking lose. The two suspects that had been at the bottom of the stairs on the tarmac had just suddenly disappeared ... right before everyone's eyes.

Officers were yelling, "Where'd they go?" and "Where the hell are they?" They were scurrying all around ... looking for some clue as to what just happened?

Agent Fisher got off the tarmac and seemed in a daze at first. Then he noticed the chaos all around. He noticed something else. He was no longer in the SUV and the SUV was gone? It had disappeared. "We're missing the SUV? They have taken the SUV Sir?" He yelled to his supervisor. "What the hell? Did they gas us?"

O'Reilly and Baxter were with other agents when the call came in from the airport.

"O'Reilly here ... are they in custody?"

"Sir ... they're gone? We had them Sir! We had them on the tarmac! Agents were closing in and ... then suddenly they weren't there! They disappeared right before our very eyes!"

"What the hell do you mean they disappeared before your eyes?" O'Reilly yelled.

"Sir … all I can tell you is we have over two hundred agents and officers here! We had them surrounded and then they were gone! And one of our government vehicles is missing! Sir … I think they are on their way to Headquarters!" The agent shouted through all the commotion at the airport.

Just then an agent burst into O'Reilly's room and yelled, "Sir … they're downstairs … the mother and the little girl! They're coming up to see you right now!" He was out of breath.

"You mean they're being escorted up to see us don't you?" O'Reilly asked.

"Not exactly Sir! Agents tried to stop her and drew their guns but … holy shit Sir … I saw it with my own eyes! Their arms are gone! She took their arms! And their legs are gone! Their arms and legs just disappeared in a microsecond!" The agent was in shock. "Sir … they aren't human! … They can't be human! … She isn't human! … I saw it with my own eyes!" And then he ran out of the room to hide.

O'Reilly ordered a "Lockdown" and all agents to action. "What the hell is going on?" He shouted to no one in particular.

At the main entrance the receptionist saw what happened to those agents as they approached the Mommy and little girl. How they dropped to the floor all at once and she saw the agent's legs and arms were … just gone! She quickly picked up the phone but just froze in shock and then the Mommy and little girl approached her.

"You can tell them we're coming up to see them … Agent Baxter and her boss. Go ahead and let them know." The little girl said with a frown on her face. The receptionist had goose bumps when the little girl spoke to her.

Caitlin had turned off all the cameras in the building. She left the phone on so the receptionist would let them know she was coming up. She tried to make the call. She couldn't. Her fingers were shaking too much to push the buttons on the phone!

Then Caitlin turned to Mommy ... looked down and saw exactly where Daddy was. Caitlin looked at Mommy again and said, "First we're going downstairs to get Daddy. That is where they have him."

They walked to the elevator and then got in and the elevator automatically went to the level Daddy was at. The elevators in this building were extremely fast. There were lots of agents ready for them. They never had a chance. The instant the door opened Caitlin froze everything in the corridor. Caitlin walked out with Mommy and turned left towards a room with big, thick steel doors ... a kind of bunker type of room. There was a window to the right with very thick bulletproof glass and Caitlin walked over with Mommy and looked in. They saw Daddy strapped to a chair. There were three interrogators inside and they looked at the window and saw the mother and the girl outside. Mommy screamed when she saw her husband like that.

Caitlin yelled and even though the room was soundproof her voice somehow entered the room as if there were no wall. "Open the door now! Let my Daddy go!"

All three just shook their head no. "We aren't opening the door!" They were not aware of what had just happened moments ago to the other agents. They just wondered how the hell did the two get into the building in this secure area? They picked up a line but the phones were now dead. Caitlin saw to that. Caitlin and Mommy walked to the big steel doors and the three agents ran to the big window to watch them from inside the room. They had their guns out. Caitlin was deciding what should she do? Entering the room would not be a problem but she wanted to enter it with a statement. Making the doors disappear? Melting the doors? Buckling the steel doors? Walking through the steel doors? She thought it best to buckle the huge steel doors ... for effect. And so the big doors started to creak ... and groan

… and bend … and buckle for just a few seconds and then the doors flung open. This time when they entered the agents fired upon them. The guns just clicked and no bullets flew. Caitlin just got rid of their legs. They lay slithering on the ground barely able to move as they called out for help … and in fear. Mommy and Caitlin ran to Daddy and Caitlin just thought about it and broke the restraints. The handcuffs and restraints were no more. They hugged him for a minute and wouldn't let go.

Mommy asked him, "Are you okay? Are you hurt? Did they hurt you Michael?"

"I'm just tired … very tired." But he managed to stand up. He had been deprived of food, water and sleep. He had some marks on his body. "I'm okay. I think I can walk. What took you so long?" He asked his daughter with a slight smile.

"Sorry Daddy. It won't happen again. I promise." Caitlin hugged her Daddy. "We're going to leave but first we are going upstairs to talk with that Baxter."

"These men and women are without arms or legs Caitlin? What's going to happen to them?" Mommy asked. Daddy looked at the three men without legs in disbelief.

"They'll get their arms and legs back after we leave but first I want to talk with Baxter." Caitlin repeated the part about going upstairs. Mommy and Caitlin helped Daddy walk. As they passed the agents that were either frozen or without limbs the parents just stared in amazement.

"How is it you can do that Caitlin? Humans can't do these things? Daddy asked.

"I'll tell you later Daddy but first we are going up to the fifth floor."

They took the elevator to the fifth floor and one could see the trail of agents and carnage along the way. O'Reilly and Baxter were in the office. They heard some reports of what was happening but there was much they didn't know.

Baxter spoke first in the room moments before they arrived. "Sir … I really think you might as well put that gun away. The ease at which they have cut a path through our best agents … entered our most secure building … and from the reports we have from Rio … I really don't think your gun is going to matter. Look outside."

O'Reilly turned to the window to look outside. The day had been bright and sunny earlier but suddenly it was ominous outside. The darkest clouds were everywhere and in the sky were several giant fiery tornados … spinning … as if they were waiting for some unforeseen command to touch down to destroy the N.S.A. Headquarters and surrounding areas. There were also reports that several fiery tornados were hovering just outside the White House in Washington D.C., as well as every other foreign government headquarters building in the World that was involved in the hunt for little Caitlin. Winds were blowing and howling and chaos was everywhere. As Baxter and O'Reilly stared outside at the doomsday sight the entire building suddenly shook like there was a giant explosion. There was no explosion though. Caitlin just moved the Earth but for a second and every living thing on the planet felt it.

And then the locked door to their room just exploded. The steel door detonated as small particles of steel shrapnel flew into the room. There was no grenade though … nor any explosive device. It was only the power of the little girl's mind. No pieces hit any occupants inside. Caitlin made sure of that. And then through the dust and smoke a little girl emerged and entered the room … she had with her a rag doll that she carried in her left hand. Behind her walked her parents … her Daddy and Mommy. O'Reilly thought better and immediately dropped his weapon and held up his hands. Baxter just stood there with her hands open … not sure what to do or what to say?

Little Caitlin walked to the window and looked outside at the darkest day in history. It was like an eclipse with a darkening of the Sun of the darkest type that befell upon Earth. Caitlin held up Sally ... her rag doll to the window and simply said, "See what happens when evil people try to do bad things Sally?" Then she turned to look at Baxter and O'Reilly and gave a dirty look. Both O'Reilly and Baxter throats instinctively gulped.

Then O'Reilly cleared his throat and said, "Look here ... I don't actually know what is going on here but ..." He never got to finish. Suddenly his mouth was gone. It was as if his lips and mouth had never been there. He had no tongue to speak and no mouth to use. Baxter screamed in terror. O'Reilly felt for his mouth and realized ... he no longer had one. Panic filled his eyes. He couldn't even mumble.

"Caitlin! Fix it!" The Mommy screamed.

Caitlin looked at her Mommy and then her Daddy ... and then O'Reilly's mouth reappeared.

"Jesus Christ!" O'Reilly yelled when he got his mouth back ... taking a big breath and looking at Baxter and then the little girl. Caitlin's face wasn't happy but it also looked disappointed.

"Shut the Fuck up Sir!" Baxter snarled at her boss. "I suggest you just listen!"

O'Reilly's eyes were wide with fear ... the kind of fear he had never known ... not even in his worst nightmares.

"Sit down and listen!" Caitlin ordered the two. They sat and put their hands on top of the large table facing the little girl who stood before them. "And just so you know ... those guns strapped under the table don't work." Caitlin stared at O'Reilly and then at Baxter. "What you do and how you act in the next few minutes is going to be the most important decision of your lives. You are to stop looking for us. You will order the reward null and void. You will state that the matter has been cleared up entirely. I want you to know I have no interest in you or your politics beyond your tracking and trying to capture us. Everything you think you know about life and reality is not what you think. I am not a danger to you ... your Country or Earth so I strongly suggest you don't make it so I am. I now know why I was put on Earth ... to watch you ... all of you ... to observe ... and to learn about your ways. And I am here to help you ... all of you. But be aware that "WE" will be watching you! You must change your ways! The wars ... the pain and suffering ... the animals ... the environment! You don't have much longer! If you don't change there will be a great cleansing of the Earth. I promise you will be extinct! All of you!"

"WE? What do you mean "WE" Caitlin?" Mommy asked.

"And what do you mean by extinct Caitlin?" Daddy added. Daddy was drinking from a water bottle he found on the table.

The little girl smiled and walked to the window. She raised her hand ... the one with Sally the rag doll in it and pointed to the sky. Then she turned her head back to look at her Mommy and Daddy. "WE!!!" The little girl emphasized. She again looked to the sky. "Extinct means no longer in existence and without life. I am seven of your Earth years old now and even now I have the intellect of millenniums of knowledge of the "WE." I am still learning ... growing ... developing ... but soon ... very soon. Even now I have the ability to change Earth for the better ... or to destroy it but that will ultimately be your decision. In the meantime I will be watching ... WE will be watching."

Then Caitlin walked over to Baxter and O'Reilly and got close to their faces and looked directly into their eyes. Their eyes stared back in fear. "Tell your President and the other leaders and the people of Earth not to fear me but to fear themselves. And do not look for me for you will not find me. But know that We walk the planet ... and We are here now."

CHAPTER 19

FINAL THOUGHTS

Caitlin then turned away and walked to where Mommy and Daddy were standing. She walked between them and put both her hands in theirs. "Time to leave now." She turned back for one final ten-second stare at Baxter and O'Reilly. It seemed like an eternity. Her brows squinted but she did not say one word. The look though sent a cold shiver down Baxter and O'Reilly's spine. Then Caitlin turned her head and walked out of the room and out of sight ... parents in hand and down the hallway out of sight. In the hallway everything was frozen in time. "Hang on tight Mommy and Daddy." And then they just vanished and disappeared as if they were never there.

Baxter and O'Reilly stared at the open entrance to the room ... wondering if she was coming back. Hoping she was gone. And then the room became less dark. Light entered the room. They both got up and walked to the window and looked outside. It was sunny again. A minute later the phone rang. The phones were up and running so that was good. And so were the cameras. No one saw the family leave the N.S.A. Headquarters building. There were agents at every exit ... the guards all saying the same thing. No one had passed by them but the family was gone.

Agent Baxter and O'Reilly stood in the room on the fifth floor in shock. Finally O'Reilly said, "Did all that just really happen Baxter? What the hell am I going to tell Weatherly ... and the President?"

"Sir ... you have to tell them everything. I will back you up and we have enough agents and evidence here to corroborate this ... whatever happened here?" Baxter looked at O'Reilly. "And one other thing Sir."

"What's that Baxter?" O'Reilly looked dumbfounded.

"Well Sir ... all this ... everything about this case ... is going to make Area 51 look and sound like a pin dropping." Baxter told O'Reilly.

"You got that right Baxter. You got that right." He repeated as he shook his head. "But even with all those witnesses the government will find a way to explain it all away. The tornados as some freakish weather event … the witnesses as some kind of mass delusion or brain washing event. They have a way of using the mainstream media to distort what actually is. I love my Country but that is the reality of how things are done … and there is another fact Baxter."

"What's that Sir?" Baxter looked at her boss.

"You know damn well the United States government isn't going to stop looking for her. That is the really scary part. I've always said if you are going hunting make sure you understand what you are hunting. They have no idea what they are hunting and that is what is going to keep me up nights. What the Hell? Cleansing the Earth? Extinct?

They both stood in silence looking at the fragments and open doorway. Thirty minutes later they all went to look at the huge, thick steel vault like doors downstairs. They saw the carnage of agents without arms or legs along the way. They stared at the vault doors that were supposed to be indestructible … impenetrable. They were made of one hundred tons of reinforced steel and granite. The steel doors now looked like crumpled tinfoil.

O'Reilly pulled Baxter off to the side. He looked back at the mangled mess of steel doors one last time. "You know Baxter … I am thinking retirement from the N.S.A. may not be such a bad idea right now."

"I know what you mean Sir. I was thinking the same thing myself." Baxter nodded her head in agreement.

Ambulances and medical personnel were called to the N.S.A. building to help the limbless as best they could. As they drove up they noticed something. All the cars in the main parking lot were … well … upside down on their roofs. Caitlin kept her promise to her parents … nobody died … at least not this time.

༽༼

Scientists all over the World confirmed that the Earth had stopped and shook for just a second. They had no idea how or why it had happened? There should have been tidal waves as an aftereffect but there wasn't? It was as if that one-second in time was lost forever. There was a great fear among the people all across the planet as no one could explain to them why the Earth had stopped for that one second, and all upon Earth had stopped with Earth as well for that one-second? Seven days later the agents that were without legs or arms suddenly returned to normal ... their limbs suddenly reappearing as if they were never gone. They all quit the N.S.A. that day. Caitlin waited those seven days so that others could see for themselves and believe what had happened. The government tried to keep it a secret.

༽༼

A millisecond after leaving the N.S.A. Headquarters a family of three suddenly materialized at the front door of a house.

Mommy and Daddy just stood tightly holding onto Caitlin's little hands. "Where are we Caitlin? What happened?" Mommy asked.

"We're in Switzerland Mommy and Daddy. I told you travelling by jet was very slow and stupid but now I know how to travel better. But before we leave there is one thing I want to do first." Little Caitlin then pushed the doorbell. She actually used her fingers rather than her mind and a few seconds later someone answered the door.

"Oh my God?" Grandpapa smiled as he opened the door. He quickly looked around ... he had a private place but he ushered them in quickly none-the-less. "I can't believe it? It is so good to see you. I wasn't sure if I would ever see you again. Are you safe?"

But first Caitlin went in for a hug. "Grandpapa." She screamed in delight and then everybody hugged. "We are safe Grandpapa. I know your stem cell work is really going good and you are on lesson three. In just a few short years you will have the cure for Alzheimer's and much more. And I know you are sharing your … our findings with your colleagues. But I came here not only to see you but to meet your wife Grandpapa."

"She's not here Caitlin." Grandpapa stated sadly.

"I know she isn't here. I know where she is. Take me to her. I want to see her. Let's go right now." Caitlin told Grandpapa.

"She's not doing so well unfortunately Caitlin. There have been some setbacks." The Grandpapa sighed. His face suddenly looked lonely.

"I know. Take me to her. Let's go in your car right now Grandpapa. Trust me." Caitlin insisted.

Grandpapa just looked at her … then at Michael and Nuwa.

Nuwa said, "Yea … let's go Lucas. Brace yourself though. I think you are about to witness another miracle. We're still trying to get used to it."

Afterwards … outside the nursing home little Caitlin stood with her parents …holding their hands and smiling. Inside Grandpapa was with his wife. He was crying tears of joy and talking to her … and she was talking back to him. He had his wife back.

Caitlin looked up to the blue sky and white clouds and thought out loud. "Well … just two more things."

"What now Caitlin?" Daddy smiled down at his little girl.

"Now don't go freaking out on me. Promise me you won't!" Caitlin looked up at her parents.

"Oh GOD! More bad news Caitlin?" Mommy asked.

"No more bad news Mommy. Close your eyes and hold my hands tight." Caitlin kind of smirked. The parents did as asked. Ten seconds later Caitlin told her parents to open their eyes. They started shrieking. They looked down at their little girl and she was someone else. Then they looked at each other and they were both someone else. She left their voices intact as they were before. "Take the mirror out of your purse Mommy and see what you look like ... you too Daddy ... check the mirror and see what you look like. I changed the cellular structure of your features so you both look totally different. If you don't like how you look I can change it." Caitlin explained. "I've changed our passports and I.D. too!"

"But I'm not even Chinese anymore Caitlin?" Mommy shrieked looking in the mirror. "And Daddy's different and you're different?"

"We're still the same inside. I read you minds ... sorry ... and changed your cellular features to a form that you would both be attracted to. If you want to be of Chinese descent I can make you Chinese anytime you want Mommy ... same for you Daddy. I could even turn myself into a boy if you wanted." She started to really giggle at that thought.

"No ... I like having you as a daughter so please don't. We are shocked enough for now." Then Daddy added, "Well ... I kind of think I am more handsome now? Don't you think so honey?" Daddy joked with Mommy as he looked in the mirror. Her mouth was wide open and wasn't closing.

"You better close your mouth Mommy … in case a bug flies in there? Caitlin was still giggling and tried not to laugh. She wasn't successful.

Mommy looked at Caitlin and then looked carefully at her husband and smirked. "Yea … well … I guess I can get used to your looks." And then winked and laughed, "How about my looks Michael?"

"Oh … I think you'll do just fine too honey." Daddy smiled at Mommy. Both were laughing now.

"Okay … good! I've actually changed our DNA slightly. They aren't going to be able to find us now no matter what. No Country will. And now for the second thing." Caitlin whispered … "Well … where would you like to go … anywhere in the World? Past or present?" Little Caitlin looked up at her parents.

"Past or present? You mean you can go into the past Caitlin?" Daddy asked.

"Yup." Caitlin responded. She couldn't stop smiling.

"Can you go into the future Caitlin? I'm just wondering?" Mommy asked.

"I can but let's stay with the past or present for now." Caitlin suggested. "I still have some more things to work out. And since I mentioned time travel perhaps I can explain it like this? I know about all the counter theories like going back in time and killing your lineage grandmother or someone so you couldn't be born. People say you can't unscramble scrambled eggs but really you can. You just need to understand and know how it can be done. Let me explain. For every dimension or concept there is a possibility of lateral movement … in many directions. For example; for every forward move there must be a backward move … for every left there must be a right … for every up there must be a down … for every inside there must be an outside … for every hot there must be a cold … for every calm there must be a wind … for every life there must be a death … for every darkness there is a light … and there are many more. People used to say man was not meant to fly and therefore he never would but he did. Then they thought the sound barrier could not be broken but it was. Kind of like you can't travel faster than the speed of light theory or what would happen if you were travelling faster than the speed of light and turned on your headlights. Well … that would just be like the Doppler effect but for light waves instead of sound waves. By the way you can travel faster than the speed of light … otherwise space travel would suck. People used to think the World was flat but they found out it wasn't and in a sense … the people on Earth today are stuck in the World is flat phase or way thinking in many areas … they just don't see it … the possibilities. They will one day … if they can survive. There is one thing that is very worrisome though Mommy and Daddy."

"What's that Caitlin?" Mommy and Daddy took a deep breath. This time Caitlin really shocked them good! What they didn't realize was that there would be even more shocks to come. That is what happens when you are the parents of a Young Supreme Being.

"That right now I can only see so far into the future and then there is nothing. That there are no people on Earth anymore … that time is running out … and it isn't that far away. I have much to do and many to educate if the People on Earth have any chance to survive what is coming." Caitlin looked out to the beauty around her with a hint of sadness.

"Caitlin … People on Earth? And what did you mean by the WE and the extinction and time running out and space travel?" Daddy asked. He looked at his little girl waiting for an explanation? Both parents were suddenly very scared?

"I know Daddy … I know. I have so much to tell you and Mommy but we need to leave first … okay?" Caitlin winked. "I can tell you both tonight … and many nights after that. Trust me and try not to worry too much."

"Okay … tonight? Well … I don't know about you Caitlin but I'm ready for a vacation." Daddy looked at his wife. "What do you think Nuwa? Are you ready for a vacation?"

"Yea … I'm definitely ready for a vacation! Where should we go? You decide Caitlin. And let's not forget about that Birthday Party!" Mommy looked lovingly at her daughter.

Daddy looked down at his little girl and said, "That's right! We have to have a Birthday Party don't we Princess? Happy Birthday Caitlin." They all did a three-way hug.

Caitlin did a little Birthday dance. "A Birthday Party," she squealed in delight as she smiled and looked up at Mommy and Daddy and purred, "I see sand … lots and lots of white sand … and beautiful blue waters … and nothing but glorious sunrises and sunsets."

Just over a year later Lynne Baxter was in her house asleep in the second floor bedroom. She lived alone after the divorce a year earlier. She didn't retire from the National Security Agency and was promoted to a Security Supervisor position and now had O'Reilly's job since he had retired after the Fort Mead incident. Lynne had decided to stay with the N.S.A. and actually dreaded the search for the little girl but she had her orders and so the government continued hunting for Caitlin. They still had the reward for her capture. There had been no sightings and they had no idea where Caitlin or the parents were on the planet. Lynne was sleeping when suddenly she was stirred from her deep sleep. She lifted her tired head from the pillow and looked about her bedroom. She was jolted to reality when she saw standing in the doorway in the moonlight the silhouette of little Caitlin looking at her. Caitlin was holding Sally … her rag doll in her left hand. Lynne quickly reached for her loaded SIG Sauer P229 that she always kept under her pillow at bedtime. It wasn't that the gun wasn't there but that she suddenly had no arms to grab it … and her legs were gone! She screamed in morbid terror as she tried to sit up in the bed. She couldn't. She screamed into the warm night air … "Caitlin! … No! Please! I'll stop! I'll stop! I promise!" Suddenly Lynne managed to sit up and looked but Caitlin was no longer standing in the doorway? She couldn't see her. Lynne realized she had her arms and legs back and she quickly rolled over and turned the light on that was atop her bedside table. A cold sweat and a chill completely enveloped her body. She reached for the P229 under the pillow and stood up shaking in fear. All was quiet. She tiptoed to the doorway and peered down the dark hallway and called Caitlin's name several times but there was no answer … only the dead silence of the night. She was breathing heavily and her heart was pounding in her chest. She stood there for a moment wondering and unsure if it was just a dream? She walked to the window to look outside into the semi-darkness of the moonlight. There was a full moon and strange clouds seemed to be surrounding the moon. She just had an eerie feeling something bad was going to happen and happen soon. The beams of moonlight shone down to Earth creating easy viewing of the area outside. Lynne kept looking out the window for any sign the little girl was there but she saw and heard nothing. She was shaking and she couldn't stop! Lynne walked over to the desk in her room … sat down in the chair and turned on the laptop. She put the gun down beside the laptop. She quickly turned and looked back over her shoulder once more towards the doorway but saw nothing. She used her password and went directly to documents. She opened the new documents folder and starting typing and put todays date at the top of the letter.

Dear Agent Tom Weatherly - Security Head Supervisor - N.S.A.

Please accept this formal notice as my resignation from the National Security Agency of the United States of America. My resignation is immediate, without prejudice, and this decision is final and without recourse. I would like to thank the National Security Agency and the United States of America for the opportunity to serve my Country.

All identification and firearms will be surrendered as per protocols immediately.

P.S. Stop looking for Caitlin before it is too late!

Sincerely,

Agent Lynne R. Baxter

Then agent Baxter printed the document … signed the letter of resignation and put it in an envelope addressed to Weatherly. She then sealed the envelope. She put the P229 in the desk drawer and placed the letter on top of the desk. She turned the chair and sat staring at the doorway to her bedroom. All she could hear was the constant ticking of the clock on the wall mixed with the pounding of her rapidly beating heart within her chest. And it made her think about time … and how time was running out for the people on Earth. It was going to be a long night … a very long night indeed.

*"The greatness
of a person is not
measured by what they
can do but by what they will do.
And I believe there is greatness in all of us,
Even The Children."*

By: Steven R. General

"And as the
mighty waves of
the ocean pound against the
white virgin pebbles of sand on the beach
...so do I."

By: Steven R. General

ACKNOWLEDGMENTS

I would like to thank the Starbucks in Parry Sound, Ontario and the Starbucks on Golf Links Road in Ancaster, Ontario. I have done much of my work at those coffee shops and enjoyed their drinks and snacks while working on storyboards and writing.

I really should acknowledge Edgar Rice Burrough and John Steinbeck. I have many favorite authors but those two especially influenced my reading and writing. When I attended my first University, I went to some yard sales in Guelph, Ontario, and it was at one of these yard sales that I noticed a box below some tables. I kicked at the box as I thought it was full of clothes but it wasn't. It was full of Edgar Rice Burrough novels that were quite old. I asked how much for the books and was told $2.00 for the box. What a find! I have treasured those books and they have affected my love of reading and writing. The imagination knows no limits and if applied neither does life's realities.

ABOUT THE AUTHOR

Steven R. General graduated with a degree in psychology from the University of Guelph and a degree in education from Laurentian University before working as a teacher, vice principal, principal, and director of education.

He has been on television three times to promote and discuss his books, which include T*he Secret Extinction: An Awakening, How to Catch Big Trout and Parrots: Wildlife and Bear Stories, G…High School was Never Like This: The Embryonic Genesis*, and the recently published *Young Supreme Being*.

General currently lives in Ontario, Canada.

You may contact the Author on Twitter: @authorsrgen
or at gmail; blueauthor.15@gmail.com

www.ingramcontent.com/pod-product-compliance
Lightning Source LLC
Chambersburg PA
CBHW051507170626
46811CB00002B/685